Books by Peter Marks

Collector's Choice
Hang-Ups

Hang-Ups

Hang-Ups

PETER MARKS

Random House New York

Library of Congress Cataloging in Publication Data

Marks, Peter.
Hang-ups
I. Title.
PZ4.M3468Han [PS3563.A667] 813'.5'4 72–11844
ISBN 0–394–48362–6

Manufactured in the United States of America

9 8 7 6 5 4 3 2

First Edition

To Walter

Hang-Ups

HER MARVELOUS breasts, engorged with silicone, reflected the soft light with a lunar whiteness. Beneath Dynel lashes, her eyes smoldered, looking straight at him, while her pink cat's tongue played somewhere behind the smile of her wet, glistening mouth. Supine on an area rug of the most luxurious acrylic plush, the curve of her hip dared poet and pornographer to define its eloquence before it careened wildly down her pneumatic thigh and tapering calf. The equilateral triangular perfection of her sex-thatch, clipped as precisely as an English hedge, was the ultimate destination of the midline of her belly, whose navel displayed a jewel formed like a rabbit's head. Frontal pubic nudity had come to *Playboy* and Sidney approved.

He flung the magazine across the bed and looked for the thousandth time at the telephone on the night table. I'm not going to be just a breather, he said to himself. But the longer he looked at the phone, and the closer he came to picking up the receiver, he became increasingly aware of his frantic heartbeat and his sprinter's breath. He was frightened that he was coming so close to doing what he had thought about all day, and reaching for the magazine again he began leafing through the pages, hoping to find some article that would command his attention and divert him from the oppressive fantasy that pursued him.

A panorama of turquoise Caribbean water caught his eye, a background to a group of broad-shouldered young sportsmen posing in blue blazers on the dock of a marina. The caption advised him to plan for winter cruises and to follow the example of those pictured— send his boat to Barbados and get his wardrobe together for winter action. Blue blazers were in; so was music. A how-to inset explained the way to fit an on-board stereo with gyroscopes to avoid distortion in make-out sounds that guaranteed success if a tropical moon and wind in the halyards were not enough inducement.

Without thinking, Sidney's fingers sought out the centerfold. Maybe she would look like that, he thought, but the idea intimidated him, and he tossed the pages over the edge of the blanket out of sight onto the floor. Perhaps she would be a *he;* that would be ridiculous. Girls didn't write obscene graffiti about men on bus seats, at least none that he knew. The inscription had been a model of clarity: *For a good hot fuck/ call 334-5688.* And guys didn't *get* fucked, they fucked, so logically the number had to be a girl. Then for a wild moment he was certain it was Mayor Lindsay's private wire at Gracie Mansion, but retreated to the position that the number was female, his recollection of the peculiar flourish to the *f* making him pause again. All day at the office, after having seen the invitation enclosed in a lopsided heart the previous night, Sidney had not been able to let go of the idea. To 334-5688 he would RSVP, and instead of working at the overstuffed in-box on his desk, he had thought of scores of prurient gambits and as many responses by frightened, disgusted and angry voices at the other end of the line.

He reached for the phone and placed it next to himself on the bed, as if taking a deliberate step toward a precipice. His hand was sweaty on the receiver and he heard the drumbeat inside him, but no warmth swelled in his groin. As he rehearsed several obscenities again —a demand, a question and finally variations that began "I want to . . ." he thought of all the women he had wanted and never spoken to, all the chances offered and refused. An old shame at his own faintheartedness triggered the mechanism of action. It wasn't a matter of sex—it was a matter of principle.

Eleven-thirty. Going to the bureau, he selected a clean white handkershief and came back to the bed, where the phone lay inert and noncommittal. Picking up the receiver and folding the cotton square over the mouthpiece, he listened to the dial tone. His forefinger began inscribing arcs with the dial: three, three, four; five, six, eight . . . He paused, wondering again who it would be. *Eight,* another eight, you chicken-shit. No, nine. It would be *nine.* She would be his alone, if it was a she. No sloppy seconds. Heartbeat. Nine. No breath, watching the dial spin back with a slight ticking hiss. Ring. Ring.

A female voice.

Breathing. "I." Hyperventilation. Receiver down.

The bedroom tilted. Out of focus. Receiver up. In
focus. Three, three, four; five-six-eight-nine. So easy.
Ring. Breath held. "How about a good hot fuck?"

• • •

Sprawled obliquely on the bed, half watching television, with a round magnifying cosmetic mirror in one
hand, tweezers in the other, she was plucking her eyebrows, supporting her weight on her elbows. As the
skin raised in a tiny eruption around each hair and then
subsided, she blinked with the quick, sharp pain. The
eye and the brow filled the mirror, enlarged and dis-
torted, and she flipped it to the flat side to see the detail
in relation to the whole. Her face never did quite come
together even in rare moments of repose. The tips of
her fingers traced the contours of the reflected cheek
on which atavistic baby-fat still withheld the promise of
an alluring hollow under the bone, in spite of the hair-
line creases that were beginning to appear on either
side of her nose. Her eyes, a very dark brown she liked
to call mink, were her best features when she wasn't too
tired. They were large, but she made them even bigger
with mascara, liner and eyeshadow, hoping to mini-
mize the other components of her face—the mouth
that had reminded somebody of a bruised fruit, and her
nose, too large, an ambiguous shape that nobody said
reminded them of anything. Once convinced that she
was not pretty at all because of the overgenerous features wedged into the allotted space, she had decided,
after several less attractive friends had married, that

she was pretty enough provided she was vigilant and attentive to signs of wear. The article in *Cosmopolitan* she had read had been absolutely clear about the question of eyebrows and one's astrological sign, but to achieve the perfection of a rainbow, for that was her curve as a Scorpio, was more difficult than she had anticipated.

To be in a state of readiness, Myrna had already finished the nails of her fingers and toes, and the bimonthly depilation of her legs. In the bathroom, after showering and an overall epidermal lubrication with a cream that smelled like macaroons, she religiously took her pill, needing to be ready for love regardless of how remote the current prospects seemed.

When the phone rang, only one eyebrow had taken on its new shape, adding to the imbalance of her face. At the first ring she immediately turned down the sound of the television, fell again across the bed, picked up the mirror so that she could watch herself talking and gauge the effect. "Hello?" Nobody there. "Hello?"

It sounded like "Hi."

"Hi." Quickly going through all the familiar male phone voices she knew or had known, she wondered whether it would be better to try to get the right name, or knowing it, say the wrong one so that the caller would begin thinking about an unknown rival. "Who is this?" she said, smiling faintly, expecting the sound of a familiar name. Reaching for the buttons at the throat of her robe, she looked at the face in the mirror. Furrows plowed in her forehead. "Hello?"

There was a curious agitation at the other end of the line, and a click. After putting down the phone and barely having time to wonder about the call, it rang again.

"Hello?" Her voice was jittery this time, trying to sound natural. Knowing something was wrong, she swung her legs to the floor, knees tight together, and sat tensely on the edge of the bed. In the brief silence that followed, she tried to prepare an aggressive tone, but the words came out loosely joined together. "Is anyone there?" What? What is he saying? How about *what?*— the final caloric expletive having no meaning in her surprise. A phlegmy sound of disgust sounded involuntarily down her throat. "Oh God," she groaned, putting down the phone and withdrawing her hand quickly, as if she had touched something leprous. On the defensive, she went quickly to the front door of her apartment to check the locks and chain. The curtains in the living room were already drawn, and returning to the bedroom, she let the blinds down and closed the slats tightly. The mirror and phone lay on the bed, and sitting down again, she took up the receiver and dialed. Waiting, she watched herself in the mirror again.

"Hi, Sylvia, it's me . . . Yeah. Okay. Listen, I'm glad I got you . . . I ought to sound funny. I just had this crazy thing happen to me . . . Well, I'm busy with my eyebrows, and the phone rings, and it's this creep . . . So wait, I'll get to that. So first I think it's somebody I know, like I'm supposed to recognize who it is by the way he breathes . . . Yeah, a breather, at first . . . So I hung up, that's what I did. Wait a sec," she said, adjusting the folds of the robe around her ankles. "What do you mean 'Is that all'! It really made me very nervous, especially when he called right back . . . Oh, Sylvia, how

do I know why I picked up the phone again. I just did
. . . So then? Then he started to talk dirty . . . Well, if
you must know, he said, 'How about a good hot fuck?'
. . . Sylvia, don't be disgusting. I mean, really, sometimes you're too much. Is that all you ever think about?
. . . No, I don't. Here I am scared out of my beanbag by
some spaced-out telephone pervert, and you're practically as bad as he is. I need a little sympathy . . . Thank
you very much; you're what I call a friend in need
. . . Do? I'm going to leave the phone off the hook for
the rest of the night, and I'm going to finish my eyebrows. If you want to be stunning, it has to hurt a little."

As they talked on about make-up and clothes, she
began absently to watch the silent drama on the television, trying to relax again into the routine of the evening. "I guess I better get to bed too. You think I ought
to call the telephone company? . . . No, I suppose they
can't . . . No, I'm going to be fine . . . It's too late, but
it's really great of you to offer. Maybe we'll see a movie
next week or something. Okay, Syl . . . I did, and the
chain too. I'll see you. And thanks . . . Hey, I wonder
who he was? . . . I'll try . . . Yeah. 'Bye."

After touching the buttons on the phone carriage and
checking for the dial tone, she put the receiver on the
bed. When the sound changed abruptly to a penetrating whine, she put it under the pillow and turned up
the sound on the television, unnerved by the quiet
shadows in the apartment and the pantomiming images on the screen. She wished Sylvia had insisted on
keeping her company, remembering when girls slept
over for the fun of it, not out of fear. How safe it had
been to giggle about a boy simply because of the way

9 ((

a cowlick fell across his face, to surrender unconditionally to the idea of love and to know the certainty that she and her friends would all become mothers watching over little Gerber babies. Later, when curious hands had traced the outlines of her burgeoning curves, her acquiescence and encouragement were not for new pleasures as much as to justify the curves themselves. The talisman of those sweet-sixteen days was with her still, a tiny gold heart locket she wore and had the habit of sucking, letting the fine chain hang at the corner of her mouth. The engraved initials had worn away long ago.

The living room, through which she passed again to check the locks on the front door, was furnished with cast-offs—little rickety tables with lathe-turned legs, brittle rattan and wicker—retrieved from Second Avenue thrift shops and out-of-the-way Salvation Army outlets where the salesladies in gray smocks came to know her by name. The clerk at the hardware store knew that she had bought another end table or rocker when she asked for another tube of epoxy and a can of white enamel. As long as it was junk in need of mending or restoration, her heart had rushed out to it, but the day she noticed in an antique shop a chair identical to one she had recently bought and realized it was no older than she was, her attention turned to house plants, which promptly became terminal on the dark window sills, leaving barren branches curling out of their little plastic pots. Undaunted, she harvested the dry leaves that fell to the floor when she was out or while she slept, to use them for a mulch, convinced that the next bit of dime-store ivy would mutate into a miraculous beanstalk.

Love would happen once, she believed, even after all the loves that came in dribs and drabs, and taking the measure of men as they came along and when she could intercept them, she would resent the complications and adjustments, retreating for respite into a more recent version of her pre-nubile world of simple romance, sentimental, secret, where a man could tell her he had known many women but none of them had mattered; and when he had been thrown from his horse and she found him lying helpless on the moors, in a tangle of gorse and sweet-smelling heather, she thought a little mouth-to-mouth resuscitation wouldn't hurt before flying away for help to the great fieldstone house, his house, that held a dark secret in the West Wing. How Craythorne Manor crouched below the lowering skies! Later, as she sat before the gilded pier glass, arranging her raven tresses in a lover's knot, the candles sputtering strangely as the wind moaned beyond the mullioned windows, she wondered about the stories in the village—what ever did happen to the *first* Lady Craythorne? Suddenly he was behind her, caressing her ivory throat with his strong hands.

Well, it turned out that the son-of-a-bitch *was* married, and his wife wasn't that crazy. As a matter of fact, he finally got around to admitting that he sort of liked her, and showed a picture of his wallet-wife, looking very put-together in a deck chair under some goddamn tree in Westport, all smiles and mock-relaxing, with arched insteps and dainty underarms. If that was his problem, if that's what he wanted, fine; so she kissed him off, hiding her disappointment with parting advice. They were lovers no more; at least they could be friends, she would say, and it was her duty as a friend to point out his deficiencies. Didn't he see that she knew him better than anyone? He didn't have to pretend with her. But he did want to pretend. They all did, refusing to be scrutinized and criticized, to be made small and ordinary.

And so they all went away, most of them before she had a chance to explain the importance of a little honest criticism in a one-to-one relationship. Some who did remain stayed long enough to tell her she was intolerant, unattractive or disagreeable; most merely said they had better forget it. One or two dared to tell her about their hopes and dreams, their kinks and insecurities, and once again she gathered up her disillusionments like brown leaves on a dusty floor.

It was nearly two o'clock before she turned off the television, sleepy enough to hope that she would not have to think about the door and the chain, and the telephone under the pillow next to her in the double bed. Finally she began to go limp, more exhausted than relaxed, and thought to herself: How could anyone be so disgusting, so sick? As Myrna slipped away into sleep, another thought, perhaps by then a dream, materialized: Do I want to marry him?

• • •

Leaning stiff-armed toward the bathroom mirror, hands planted on the porcelain rim of the sink, his striped pajamas looking like reused gift wrapping, he saw the same face studying himself, no slobbering monster who could barely hold the frothing test tube, no hirsute creature brought to life by the full moon—only the same unspecific niceness, the skin-colored complexion, hair-colored hair, the subdivisions of space as conventional and diagrammatic as a surburban development, a face that, in spite of the adventure of the night before, held as few surprises for others as it did for himself. He had hoped at least to see a slight furtive cast to his eye or a new sensual curve to his lip.

Was that all there was? Was that all? Nothing more than to have exhaled after holding his breath for nearly four decades, to have breathed into a telephone, to know that his one unsubstantial moment of freedom had already been computerized and would be recorded on his monthly statement.

She would have to understand; he would make her understand. Having felt guilty at other times, he decided it would be appropriate to feel that now. She'd want that, and Sidney liked to do what was expected of him. But it was not enough that he accused and convicted himself, he had to learn the specific charge against him. From the meager evidence of her brief response, it was possible to know how much she feared him, the quality of her repugnance, what punishment she would devise. Having affected her excited him, and Sidney contemplated telling her that she wielded a power equal to his own—his victim would become his executioner. Willingly he gave her a hood and an ax, put his head on the block and looked down into the basket.

But first he would explain; he was entitled to a few last words: "I'll never do it again." That's what you said the last time. "But I'll cry for you," he went on, his eyes filling like tumblers under a faucet. If you don't stop crying, I'll really give you something to cry about. "I'm sorry," he said, concluding his summation. Apologizing had worked for him before and he would try it again.

Sidney looked at his watch. He had six minutes to go, and passed the time hoping she would know it was he when her phone rang at exactly eleven-thirty, that he would be able to detect a note of preparation in her voice when she answered. Dialing the first six digits, he paused, impatiently following the second hand on his watch as it crept through the last moments. He spun the dial to the nine with a decisive executive gesture and waited as he heard the first ring, then a second.

"Hello?" The voice sounded tentative and suspicious.

Realizing that he had forgotten the handkerchief over the receiver, he grabbed a corner of the sheet and clamped it in place. He spoke quickly. "I called you last night. Wait. Don't hang up. I've got to explain. Wait. Couldn't you . . ."

"Couldn't I what?" she asked, her voice cold and authoritative.

"I've got to explain that I'm sorry. I never did anything like that before. Let me talk to you. Please."

"You are a creep," she said with finality. "And if you don't get off the phone this second, I'm going to call the police."

"I swear to God, this is the first time I ever did anything like that."

Click. "I swear." The whole truth and nothing but the truth, he thought, raising his hand to seal the oath.

• • •

A jumble of photographs and frayed albums was spread about her on the floor: crumbling drugstore-developed Kodak snapshots going brown and silvery— of robed graduates, brides and grooms, a smiling baby who had become a chiropractor, and herself squinting into the fading sunshine. Sometimes she now saw the same tight look around her eyes as she prepared to meet the days, after dreams had opened other albums of images that never faded, that did not give off the sweet-woody smell of childhood and rotting paper.

The mementos lay scattered around her while she sat cross-legged holding a scrapbook with torn padded covers and moldering black pages, from which she was cutting photographs still stuck to the dry newsprint. Based on dated photos, Myrna was carefully arranging her chronology, documented by class and Brownie pictures. Luckily, a few camp pictures firmly dated her physical development, because most of the other photographs of her were taken by her parents on the occasion of the first wearing of a new outfit, always warm and bulky regardless of the season, it seemed to her, that her mother bought purposely (she thought) to obscure the outlines of her body. Daddy was in fur (a fur consultant, he said), and not a few of the winter coats had the same bits of Persian lamb tacked on to the collars and cuffs. The squinting smile was the same up to the age of twelve, at which point three years of tight lips elapsed. She had torn up the only picture of herself with braces, after picking up the prints at the drugstore to find that her entire face was obscured in a blinding effulgence that had reflected off one of the steel caps in the front of her mouth.

When her parents had moved to Sarasota two years before, she had asked if she could keep the box of memorabilia; a life so rich in incident needed to be arranged, annotated and explained. When she was in love, these archives lay in the closet behind her shoes, but when she was out of love, she would squat down and struggle to bring out the large corrugated box, taking up where she had left off, a day, a week or a month before, to begin again solving the problems of interpolating aunts, uncles and cousins with her own chronology.

Her parents called her once a week from Florida, and the project provided a common ground between them now that almost all other topics had become forbidden. They didn't like to think of her alone in New York; from the anxious imaginings they expressed to her, she knew her life was much worse, in their terms, than they ever dreamed. And she didn't want to think about them sitting in the sun, waiting to die. In moving, her parents had taken another step toward death, and she wondered how long it would be. It was not the grief she feared, but being alone. If she was not married before they died, she would not only be a spinster, but an orphan in the bargain.

As her mother had been an indiscriminate saver, there was much sorting to do. Restaurant matchbooks, resort-hotel menus, postcards, a headline for V-J Day, and other irrelevancies had to be weeded out. Her parents were her only source of oral history. The few calls made to married cousins for information and dates had been disastrous. If there were only husbands, there was an endless gush of exclamations of how well Marvin, or Arnold, was doing, and how housework wasn't work at all but positively a calling; if there were babies, it was even worse. And then the inevitable question, guarded, tinged with pity, about what was happening to her? The date of Aunt Lillian's marriage to Morris simply wasn't worth the strain, and as far as Lillian and Morris were concerned, the only time she had called them, they called her parents and told them some absurd story about her getting engaged, when all she said was yes, she was seeing somebody, at which point her parents called her, asking tearfully why they had to hear about it from strangers. The work went slowly as she examined each document and photograph for meanings. Still unopened in its Tiffany box was the new album she had ordered, fit for a papal library.

Myrna was concentrating on a particularly difficult cross-pollination in the family tree: a widowed cousin on her mother's side had married her father's sister-in-law's brother, and produced a child. Myrna had formerly been too impatient with the problem of whether to consider the offspring a cousin in some sort of degree, first, second or third, or to define the baby in terms of a relative from whom she was removed, once, twice or thrice. Tonight she had decided to review her decision simply to consider the unlucky baby an undefined pain in the ass because it distracted her from watching the progress of the clock through the night toward eleven-thirty. He had called twice. Was he a second-degree lover or a lover twice removed? The door was already double-locked and chained, the blinds down and the curtains drawn.

The jolt of the ringing startled her. She rose defiantly and stared at the phone as though it were alive—demanding, wanting her—and Myrna knew she had hoped it would ring. Smiling, she began to count; he loves me, he loves me not . . . seven times. He loves me. Then silence. Kneeling on the floor and reaching across the photographs to the glossy light-blue box, she removed the new album, and after feeling the fine cool leather, began leafing through the blank pages.

•　•　•

"Wait," commanded the voice.

I'm not going anywhere, she thought. "Do I know you? I mean, did I ever go out with you or something?"

"No." There didn't seem to be any further questions or answers.

"Listen, just say you're sorry, like a nice little pervert, hang up and don't bother me again," she said, trying to sound bored.

"Well, I am sorry. But I couldn't help it. I'll never do it again."

"Just don't do it to me."

"I didn't mean to frighten you."

"I'm not afraid of you. I pity you. If you want to know the truth, I find you very disgusting."

"You shouldn't be afraid."

"I *told* you I'm not afraid. Oh Christ, what the hell am I talking to you for?" As Myrna realized she expected an answer, she hung up.

• • •

We actually had a conversation, Myrna thought, trying not to believe what had happened. He said, then I said, then he said; I'm sitting here talking to a maniac. What else do I have to do, she wondered, looking at the photographs and scrapbooks spread out on the floor. As she was about to take the phone off the hook, she changed her mind. Nobody is going to tyrannize me, she resolved. The next time he calls . . . The *next* time? I must be going crazy too. She slipped the little heart locket into her mouth, sucking it like a lozenge, and returned to her work. The names of her senior high school class were written on the back of the photograph she held. They were all cheese-smiling directly into the camera, except for herself, staring now at the white margin of the paper.

Remembering that she had been told she had spoiled the picture, she thought of the beach that day, their class outing, and the new aqua Esther Williams Jantzen and how they had all shown off their city-white bodies to each other, self-conscious in the revelation of their armpits and toes, erotic in their exposure. From the safety of the herd she had lain on the blanket looking outward and saw him lying on his back, taking the sun full in the face. She shaded her eyes, as if he were radiating light, and watched the steady rhythm of his abdomen as he breathed the heat. How could anyone be so beautiful, she wondered, and as if in response to her gaze he stirred, raising his torso on one elbow, adjusting his bathing suit and lazily running his palm over his sweating chest, loitering in the briar of hair that sprouted between his pectorals. He wants me, she had thought in a moment of thrilling terror; I'm going to pass out. He waved, kneeled and got up, and then she saw another girl stepping lightly between the blankets whom he met and drew down to him. Everybody was grouping for the picture and she had obediently faced the camera, baring her teeth. In the long interval while the photographer's finger paused on the button, she could not resist turning to accuse the man who had betrayed her. There was a burst of laughter and a collective movement of close bodies and it was all over.

His first call had been an isolated incident without meaning, as if a photograph of a stranger had turned up in the box of pictures and distant voices. But since he tried to explain, it meant that he had thought about her, that she figured in his life. He had given her a new dimension. The voice sounded far away and muffled, but she could hear the urgency of its need to explain itself to her. They had a future.

Myrna first became conscious of time stretching before her when she saw the proofs of her college year-book pictures. The smiling one she selected was the terminus of the past, after which she kept no records. The events between then and now were an accumulation of sensations and memories that were stored in disorderly nests. When she thought she was in love she would begin to try to find a pattern, fashioning a past that had led her to her lover, as surely as a lost child in a fairy tale had found an enchanted cottage deep in a wood. But the magic had always vanished long before she reached her destination, and the pattern had become choked with weeds and the wood was again dark and impenetrable. Everything that had happened to her since that day when she had put on the string of pearls and cocked her head, just so—the jobs, the dates, the two-week vacations, the one-night stands—was still part of the future. She stood behind it all, pushing it before her, an immense offering to an unknown lover who would look at the whole tottering juggernaut of memories and bric-a-brac and receive it as a gift worth a king's ranson, realizing that each detail, however anomalous, was part of her and therefore precious to him. Until that investiture, she would not look too closely at what she was offering, in case there might already be a hidden meaning she might find herself. It would be better to leave the knots loosely tied and the joints unglued. He would do the tying and the joinery for her. The present was a makeshift affair, a temporary inconvenience while she was in the process of creating herself.

The phone rang at eleven-thirty the next night. To

test him, she had not taken the box out of the closet that evening.

"Hello?"

"Please don't hang up. It's me again."

"I'll give you exactly thirty seconds to explain what is going on in your so-called mind."

"Don't be frightened."

"You've got twenty-five seconds to go."

"I don't even know your name or where you live." A puzzled silence devoured another piece of his time. "I didn't get your number from the telephone book, if that's what you think."

"But I don't understand," she said. "Wait a minute. You're just trying to get me off guard. Well, forget it, because there's a twenty-four-hour doorman and closed-circuit television. Besides which, when I hang up on you, I'm going to call the telephone company and have my number changed."

"You needn't bother, because honestly, I don't know anything more than your number."

"Somebody told you to call me."

"No," he answered, as if she had said something incredibly stupid.

"Just out of curiosity, how did I get to be your lucky number? Make it snappy though; you're talking on borrowed time."

"I looked you up in the Yellow Pages under 'V' for 'Victim.'"

"A sex maniac with a sense of humor." She paused. "Okay, the guessing game is over. Now, where did you get my number?" she demanded, making the anger rise above her curiosity.

"From a bus," he answered.

"A bus told you my number," she said. "A *bus* told him my number," she explained to an invisible third person. "You see, this guy I never met, who turns out to be a perverted freak, also talks to buses. No, really. I'm serious. Wait, I'll ask him. Hey, Freak, was it the Twenty-third Street Crosstown?"

"Please don't."

"He said, 'Please don't.' Maybe it was the Madison Avenue Number Four. It's so chic. Yeah, I'll ask him. Hey, Freak, was it the Number Four? Hey, Freak! *Freak!*" Still keeping the receiver next to her ear, she pressed the button on the phone carriage as if it were a vital pressure point. She released the button, but the line was dead.

• • •

"Hello, it's me Sidney." There was no answer, but she didn't hang up either. "Just give me a chance to finish what I was saying. I'm not what you think I am at all."

"I don't think you're anything. I mean I think you're nothing."

"Well, that's something at least. I've got to explain. I'm not an obscene phone call."

"What are you, a singing telegram?" she said. "Was that bit about the bus really true? My number was written on a bus?"

Once Sidney had told a girl she was pretty, yet after her eyelids had fluttered she had asked whether he really meant it. There was only one response to both demands for reiteration, but of what now? Not only the safety of her anonymity, he knew. Without knowing her reason, Sidney felt she needed it to be true, and said, "In a sense."

"What's that supposed to mean?"

"I was on the Lexington Avenue bus coming home very late," he began.

"You should have taken a cab, you cheapskate," she said. "Very creepy people ride the buses at night."

"Two creepy people by dawn's early light," he sang, "and too much in love to say goodnight."

"You've got the worst voice I've ever heard."

"You can't tell, because I've got this handkerchief over the receiver. I saw it once in a movie; it's supposed to disguise your voice."

"That's absurd. We'll never meet and we haven't ever met. Or have we? Listen, this isn't some kind of put-on?"

"No, I swear. It was on the Lexington Avenue bus. It was late and I was depressed, so I thought I would take the bus because I knew a cab wouldn't cheer me up, and I'd had such a lousy time the whole night, I wanted to make the trip home all of a piece. It wasn't a question of money." Trying to have an affair with a divorcée was impossible, especially one who lived uptown and had a five-year-old son. It was a waste of time, but so was everything: television, acquaintances, and the work he never failed to bring home from the office even if he knew he would not so much as open the briefcase. He had sat next to it on the bed, shining his shoes before going out, when she had called to say that the baby-sitter had reneged and they would have to stay in. The kid sleeping in the bedroom had gotten up six times for a bottle, and kept asking who he was.

"Once I got so depressed," Myrna said, "I went into Schrafft's and ordered ravioli. It looked like chopped tapeworm marinara. Go on."

"So I was sitting on the bus looking at the ads telling me to give to these various loathsome diseases." It was after one in the morning when he had boarded the empty bus at Ninety-sixth Street, and still cold in the poplin raincoat he had mistakenly worn that evening, he slumped in his seat, looking at the pleading slogans, pictures of the sick, the addicted and deformed, the abandoned and the old. When she had called, the idea of a domestic scene had appealed to him, and he thought it would be nice not to sit in the crowded restaurant in the Village and joke about whether either or both of them would eat garlic or not. But it wasn't nice at all.

Over the scrambled eggs and tired leftovers, hunched over her coffee table, the silences were oppressive without the accustomed canned music and the bits of other people's conversations that often made them smile at each other when neither of them had anything to say. "And when I got to cancer," he said, "there wasn't any picture, but they gave you a list of ten possible symptoms, any one of which meant that you had a fairly good chance of being dead within six months." He considered himself a perfect specimen when he flexed before the mirror, if he didn't look too closely at the incipient flab and a crust of dandruff now and again. "The trouble was," he continued, "that a couple of the symptoms were so vague, like frequent

25 ((

headaches. I mean, I get headaches, but what is *frequent?*" The sex book his father had given him on the eve of his adolescence took the liberal view that it was okay to play with himself as long as he didn't do it too frequently, but leaving the qualification to the dictates of his conscience and glands had been a troublesome, unresolved dilemma.

"It's anxiety and tension," Myrna said, dismissing the threat of his imminent death as well as minimizing the importance of his pain. "The only thing you've got to do is to put your life in shape."

"Is that all? Gee, and I thought it was something serious," Sidney said. He had sat on the bus wondering about himself. All he could see were small pieces of a puzzle, none of which had a straight edge or corner, so that he couldn't tell where they were supposed to fit or what the fragments indicated about the whole. Blue could be sky or water; the broken lines and bits of color were inexplicable. He tried occasionally to match the strange shapes together, moving them about, frustrated, quick to anger.

"If you went to the doctor," Myrna said, "and he told you that you weren't going to die of cancer, you'd be happy. So be happy."

The demanding strips of advertisements became intolerable and he had looked toward the rear of the bus, watching the moving lights of the avenue slide backward toward a dark vanishing point. Listening to the asthmatic downshift of the bus, he rubbed the side of his cheek, feeling the rasp of his morning beard, and then explored the inner corners of his eyes for secretions that would turn into granules of sleep. Sidney liked to plan ahead. He checked a passing street sign; twenty more blocks to go, and the thought of his bed, which he always made before leaving in the morning, promised relief. Come on, he admonished himself, first of all, just because it had been one of those nights, there was no reason to be so down on himself. Didn't he live in a new building near Gramercy Park? An apartment with alcoves? Wasn't he a junior partner? And didn't the cleaning lady come twice a week? So don't be stupid. Aimlessly, he began to explore the tangle of graffiti at the back of the bus.

"I'm not going to die of bubonic plague either, and that doesn't make me happy. Anyway, I only go to the doctor for my hay-fever shots."

"You'd have to be allergic."

"Not until August, and this is only October. I should have worn my overcoat that night; they don't give you any heat on those buses," he complained, "and I'm feeling coldy."

"Poor baby," she commiserated, "you're a mess."

"If you think I'm a mess, you ought to have seen that bus—that spray can and Magic Marker stuff all over the walls and ceiling and windows. All those names and numbers—what kind of an ego trip is that? It's disgraceful. I mean, after all, it's public property."

"So am I, from what you said."

"Actually not," Sidney replied.

Her voice hardened. "You mean it wasn't true?"

"Yes, it's true in a sense. You remember I said, 'In a sense.' There was a telephone number, but when I decided to call, I changed the last number from an eight to a nine. I felt so out of control, I had to do something.

Believe me, it wasn't an easy thing to do, and I had an awful sort of hangover the next day."

"My Day: A Sex Maniac Tells All, by I. C. Crotchmore."

"Please don't start that again. Besides, girls shouldn't talk like that."

"Mercy me, I think I'm going to have a spell." Click.

•   •   •

"It's Sidney. Before you say anything., I'm going to make you an all-inclusive apology, a package deal: twenty percent off the retail price for guilt. I'm *sorry.*"

"Deeply sorry?"

"I'm sorry I frightened you. I'm sorry I annoyed you. I'm sorry I disgusted you. But I'm not actually sorry I called, except in the sense that I know I shouldn't have, if you know what I mean."

"Don't worry," Myrna replied, "I'll make you sorry you called."

"I personally think you're probably very nice basically. Underneath that thin veneer of hostility, you're just a very nice human being."

"Underneath that thin veneer of hostility is another veneer of hostility."

"Well, I am genuinely sorry, and I think you might have a little sympathy for the way I felt. I was very upset after that first call."

"Past tense? You mean now you feel fine. Boy, you've got one hell of a nerve."

"I'd like to know how long guilt is supposed to last."

)) 28

"How should I know? My conscience is clear."

"The worst part was the morning after, waking up with the sun shining," Sidney said.

"So far I don't hear anything about your guilt," Myrna said. "You're losing me."

"Wait, I'll get to the good part," he said. "I couldn't go to work I felt so crummy." He had dressed quickly and without shaving or brushing his teeth had left his apartment, walking south on Third Avenue in the chilly sunshine, feeling wonderfully free, delinquent, but after nine o'clock his confidence failed him. At the Bowery, where the bums stood unsteadily, blinking and confused, he went into a bar stinking of beer and disinfectant and called the office. "So I called the office and told them I had a cold," he said, remembering the shapeless derelicts downing eye-openers while he described his symptoms.

Myrna yawned loudly. "It's not that I don't find this confession positively fascinating, but I'm sleepy and I've got a thousand things to do before I go to bed. I'll tell you what I'll do: I'm going inside and make a cup of tea, and while I'm doing that, you tell me all about it. It doesn't matter whether I listen or not. It's the catharsis that's important. Okay?"

Before Sidney could answer, he heard the receiver bang against a table. He lay on his bed, remembering a tweedy couch on which he had once made a tentative experiment with psychotherapy. Fifteen years before, he had begun by saying he didn't feel anything, and had filled the rest of the first and last fifty-minute hour with a disjointed appointment calendar of a typical day, a description of events floating like icebergs on a sea, and he, adrift among them, unable to fathom or express anything beneath the surface other than the idea that the reality of his life, his awareness of the passage of time, the fact of his perceptions and changes of mood logically suggested that something unseen was there.

"Then I took a long walk and had lunch," he said. He reached the Battery and found a place where he could sit on the pilings and look down into the water churning around the blackened, upright logs, inspecting the regurgitations of the harbor, the opalescent sheen of the marine oils and the white mermaids, used rubbers floating on the swells. After a hot dog washed down with an orange drink he gave out a gaseous belch and watched the parade of secretaries gossiping and taking the sea air. He lolled on a bench in Battery Park long after the lunchtime tourists had departed into the backdrop of office buildings. Soon he was looking into the smoking sunset as the cloudy dregs settled on the horizon.

His one-shot doctor had said, staring beyond him at the expensive view of Central Park, that he ought to open up a little more. The whole truth and nothing but the truth.

"And then everybody seemed to be going home from work and I got into the subway with them. You'd be amazed how relieved I was, since I'd lied to my office, but once I had gotten on the train, I realized I had taken the wrong IRT."

When the train came into Fourteenth Street, a brief respite from the flickering pillars and shattering noise, Sidney prepared to get out, but he was on the West Side, and not wanting to face the open streets just then, let another wave of bodies press him firmly in place; he would go to Forty-second Street, shuttle over and go down Lex. The train shuddered out of the station into the black tunnel, lumbered ahead and with an inexplicable shriek, stopped dead. Another express rushed down the track in the opposite direction, and as the seismic vibrations echoed away, Sidney watched the dead faces with cataract eyes, resigned and powerless.

You've got to begin by being more aware of your feelings, Dr. Grossbart had said. "You can imagine how nervous I felt the whole day, after what I'd done," Sidney said, still not quite sure what it was he *had* done but giving his guilt the benefit of the doubt, "and when the train got to Times Square, I got off."

The air was dank and warm with human odors, noxious as a mine shaft, and Sidney belched a poisoned memory of his lunch. He struggled toward the door before the train reached Forty-second Street, feeling the packed crowd contract behind him like the waters of a swamp closing behind a fugitive. Strangling for air, he pushed his way through the waiting passengers on the platform, hurried to the nearest staircase, and rather than following the arrows to the shuttle, turned almost at a run in the direction marked: *To Street.* Past the subterranean pizza stands, news counters and penny arcades, he bounded up the stairs into the chill night. Not a trace of the sunset remained as he leaned against the wall, sweating, looking at the gerrymander sky through the signs and marquees.

Remember, you're under oath. "It's ridiculous," he said, "the buses are too cold and the subways are too hot, so I decided to get a little air again."

Breathing heavily to rid himself of the underground vapors, Sidney had begun to walk, his hands plunged deeply into his pockets and folded in front of him, drawing the coat close to his body. He stopped in front of a bookstore, brilliantly lit with livid fluorescent fixtures, the broad display windows lined with stained crepe paper scattered with paperbacks. Perverts, he thought, my kind of people, as he surveyed the perspective of receding racks and silent browsers. Ordinary people taking little holidays, just like me. But how many did what I did, he wondered with satisfaction. Maybe they've done worse, or better.

Edging toward the door, he entered, automatically glancing at the proprietor seated on a dais, disappointed that he didn't even notice his entrance, much less shake a finger at him. Unjudged, Sidney sidled down the aisle, unable to stop anywhere in the erotic supermarket, passing through heterosexuality to the nether regions of unusual couplings and unlikely orifices. I know what you are and what you do, he thought, looking at the other customers, who observed a Trappist silence as they each read their curious breviaries.

"It's a very sick scene around Times Square, and it's funny, but I thought you'd think that's where I usually . . ." hung out, he thought, "went, and that's when I started to feel really sorry."

Deciding he could begin with relatively innocuous Scandinavian nudism, he was about to make a selection when an announcement from the dais issued the reminder that everything was for sale, and during the brief store-wide flurry of activity, Sidney darted quickly through a dark opening into the film department. Huddled figures occupied every peep-show booth as he moved warily toward the rear, and finding the last space empty he went in, resting in the silent crib. He had no intention of looking at the movie, but another man peered into the booth, and seeing him unengaged, looked as if he might join him. In a panic, Sidney turned toward the binocular viewer, and reaching for a quarter, inserted it into the mechanism identical with the one at the laundromat he went to with his sheets and pillowcases. As the soft whirring began, he pressed his eyes to the viewer, seeing a tight pelvic scene, a smear of hair, slow-motion heaving. As the camera drew back, it revealed the owner of the parts and her companion, who, from all indications, was as unimpressed as Sidney with what he saw. After a lethargic and unconsummated entanglement, the picture abruptly stopped, promising more with the insertion of another quarter. The would-be intruder made another halting effort at contact, and Sidney, seeing the pathetic, demanding question in his eyes, brushed past him toward the light.

Feelings, the Good Doctor had said, were an important way of getting to our fantasy material, and that is where we will be doing our most important work. "And so," Sidney went on, "I knew I had to call you again, to explain, that is."

Sidney divided three minutes into the time of a feature-length movie, then multiplied by twenty-five cents and decided he wasn't getting his money's worth. The familiar faces of secretaries and clerks, executives and office managers were scarcer now as he walked, the street giving over to night prowlers, grim searchers and curious sightseers. A sensual craving stirred in him as he recalled the soft-focus vignette in the peep-show cubicle. The signs and lighted buildings hung like gargantuan chandeliers above him as he turned up Broadway.

Fabulous Femmes plus Groove Tube, and Selected Featurettes. No stills outside; that was encouraging, Sidney concluded, but Jesus, suppose somebody he knew saw him going in. He put his hand to his face, pretending to scratch the bridge of his nose. Stepping into a nearby doorway, he took five dollars from his billfold, not wanting to pause at the ticket booth, wishing he had left his wallet home so that when the vice squad stormed the theater, he would be able to give a fictious name, and thinking the first thing he would do inside would be to check where the exit signs were. He thought of the magic smell of upholstery and popcorn as he approached the booth, clutching the five-dollar bill in his fist jammed to the bottom of his pocket.

The ticket girl didn't notice him at first, intent as she was on knitting a pink baby bootie, and when Sidney saw, to his horror, her large belly crowded into the tiny space, he drew back, bumping into a brawny policeman. The uniformed officer did not take the slightest notice of him as Sidney drew aside, but bent down and said through the slot, "Standing room only?" and laughed. The girl's dull face brightened, and she produced a wet fart with her outstuck tongue. Sidney withdrew further to read the titillating warning about explicit sex on the door of the theater, as absorbed as if he were reading the fine print of a contract. The cop ambled off and the girl returned to her prenatal crafts while the lights crawled around the marquee.

))34

We have a lot of hard work ahead, Sidney; I hope I
may call you Sidney, Dr. G. had asked. "I'm just a regular person," Sidney said in defeat, lying on his bed,
waiting for Myrna to return. He could still feel the
brass-buttoned obstacle, New York's finest, as tactile
and corporeal as his own humiliation, and the acid
laughter telling him he was just another horny sucker.
"Are you through?" she asked suddenly.
I've got some more, he thought. "But I still feel
guilty," Sidney said, trying to please.
"You make it sound like that makes everything all
right. Christ, some people think they can go around
doing whatever they goddamn please, as long as they
feel guilty afterwards. What about me? Don't you think
I have feelings too? You're obviously totally incapable
of having a real relationship with anybody. What you
need is help. Professional help. You do know that you
are very sick," she said, emphasizing the extent of his
illness. "It's not normal, what you did."
He had finally maintained to himself that his only
problem was finding someone who understood him.
The thought comforted him when he couldn't go to
sleep and when he had bad dreams, when he was occasionally impotent or when he came too quickly.
"What's normal?" he asked, trying to remember all the
days he had justified to himself.
"Normal is not making obscene phone calls."
"I'm just a plain, ordinary, walking psychotic," he
said. "Nobody really knows what they're capable of
until they decide to find out." That sounded more he-
roic to him.
"Yeah, but you didn't decide. You were out of con-

trol. You told me. Big deal; what do you want, a medal? If I were you, and thank God I'm not, I would have my head examined. I ought to, now that I think about it. Here I am talking to a dirty old man who should be chained to a bedpost at Rockland State."

"I'm not old."

"At least you didn't say you weren't dirty. That means you have a shred of conscience left. When they catch you, you'll only be able to plead temporary insanity. They'll say you could distinguish between right and wrong."

Sidney was struck dumb by the thought that he would actually be caught. His bedroom seemed to close in around him.

"As a matter of fact, while you've been running off at the mouth about your precious psyche, this call was being traced. I dare you not to hang up. You haven't got the guts to stay on the phone."

"You're kidding."

"Am I? Wait and see. When I called the phone company, I told them you'd call at eleven-thirty on the dot, and they told me they'd only need three minutes. It's eleven fifty-six now. Sleep well," she whispered. Click.

• • •

As it approached their time, Myrna wondered if she had gone too far. If she repaid him in kind for the fear he had insisted she feel, she would be satisfied, for the moment. But perhaps she had scared him away altogether, and she admitted that she would be disappointed. They had unfinished business, although she was not quite sure what it was. He had, in a sense, invented her, the way lovers had always invented each other. Whatever uneasiness or threat Myrna had felt had passed away. The brass chain on the door hung unattached to the jamb, and through the bedroom window she could see a small slice of cold sky.

She believed him, and believing, found a new sense of safety, of strength, and she began to feel beautiful. They were as anonymous as the faceless shadows in a confessional, and she, wrapped in a black domino, would put her mouth to the lattice and admit to acts of otherwise inexpressible sensuality, following one another in a torrent of episodes so ravishingly pleasurable that Sidney would cry out, absolving every sin if only she would stop. And now Sidney—she knew his name —now Sidney might be her confessor, not by virtue of his saintliness, but because he could match every mad yearning of hers with one of his own. They both had a calling. And he would never tell, because people like that never did. Besides, even if he did, he didn't know who she was. She could be free with him, freer than she had been with anyone else.

When he called again, it would mean that he wanted her more than he valued his own safety, his own freedom. If he would jeopardize that, make the supreme sacrifice, his call would be a gift of love. One moment with her, that extra moment, would be paid for by his watching the distant sun for a brief hour every day through the barred window of a prison cell. If he would do that for her, she would wait, and would answer; that was the least she could do. Fingering her gold heart, she resolved to have her portrait taken in miniature, painted on an ivory plaque, have it set in the locket by a little man she knew on Forty-seventh Street and smuggle it to him in a seeded roll.

Myrna spoke his name with unutterable longing, wishing it could have been Gerold or Edward. Names notwithstanding, she could forgive him everything else. Fear was part of love. So was madness, so was hope. But if he was as crazy as she said he was, then he could not decide to call, but rather merely respond to a compulsion to do so. And then he would want to be caught, punished. Fortunately, she had told him he had a conscience. It was so, and he could make a choice. He had chosen her, and she would show him that he was loved.

As the time of their assignation drew nearer, she put on a dark robe over her nightgown, combed her hair, and imagined herself gliding through a Stygian night toward a chink in a wall and her lover's voice, not thinking about love, but only whether he would be there. Calling the phone company for the time, she replaced the receiver, corrected the clock next to her bed, set the alarm and waited. There was a simultaneous ringing.

"Hello?"

"Hello, it's me Sidney."

"Hello," she said, attempting to sound indifferent, but it seemed to her as if she had said "I do." She would not repeat his name.

"I didn't sleep so well last night. I didn't sleep at all."

"Maybe it was your guilty conscience," she replied.

"Did you really have the call traced?"

"The feeling of being pursued and trapped isn't very nice, is it?" Not waiting for an answer, she continued. "I want you to know that I can do it any time I want."

"I could tell them that *you* were the one who made the call, and that *you* said that if I didn't call back, *you'd* call them and tell them it was *me.*"

"You know, people who use the word 'them' the way you do usually have a little problem. It's called paranoia. You're nutsier than I thought. Who would possibly believe you?"

"With these Women's Lib types around, a lot of people."

"Naturally you'd be anti-Women's Lib. Women are so threatening to you that you can't even have a pre-Lib, old-fashioned, role-playing relationship. If you really wanted to help yourself, you'd begin by taking that insane handkerchief off the phone. And you've got to accept the idea of the consistency of the unconscious, that everything you do is all connected. You've got the Perverted Male Chauvinist Pig Syndrome. Oink!"

"Don't be that way."

"I can just see what you look like: fat with sort of grayish-white skin and little watery eyes behind very thick glasses. And an awful pursed mouth."

"You're getting me confused with the Mad Bomber."

"And pimples."

"I used to have pimples."

Again the sound of disgust went over the wire like static. "I don't want to hear about it, or anything." But she did. "Save it for the shrink."

"I wish you'd stop going under the assumption that I'm crazy. What have I actually done to you?"

"You attacked me, just as if you'd held a knife to my throat."

"You have a tendency to overdramatize. Anyway, let's assume that I am crazy. Craziness affects people either one or two ways: either they get nervous because it reminds them of their own hang-ups, or they get smug about how normal they are."

"I hadn't thought about it one way or another, except when it affects me. Take you, for instance. I couldn't care less what your scene is, only this time I got involved," Myrna said, carefully denying her own acquiescence.

"What's your name, anyway," he asked.

"None of your business."

"That's a dumb thing to say."

"You're getting pretty uppity. You ought to be grateful that I even talk to you. I bet you don't have a single friend—except other perverts, or course. You ought to start a club: Sex Fiends Anonymous."

"You've been home every night I called."

"What's that supposed to mean?"

"You tell me."

"It means that I just got home from having dinner with this gorgeous, brilliant, rich, divine person," she said, looking at the photographs spread on the floor beside the bed.

"What does he call you?"

" 'Darling.' "

"That's very brilliant."

"I'll tell you one thing. You'd better shape up, or I'm hanging up."

)) 40

"Just tell me your name, your first name."

"I don't want to. Let's leave it at that."

"I've got to call you something. I can't go on thinking of you as three, three, four; five, six, eight, nine."

"You can call me Three Three for short."

"Give me a clue. At least a first initial."

"M."

"Margaret?"

"As in Princess?"

"No, as in O'Brien."

"Thanks. You go to the movies a lot, don't you?"

"Not particularly."

"It's another escape from reality."

"What's so great about reality?"

"You like to be in the dark so that you can be alone with your fantasies. That's very infantile."

"You ask me a question and then when I answer it you ignore what I say and make some statement that has nothing to do with what I told you."

"You're in no position to criticize me, particularly when I'm trying to help you."

"I didn't realize that's what you were trying to do."

"I think I'll watch the Late Show."

"What do you want from me?" he asked.

Oh, Sidney, if you only knew. Verses about my eyes, my breasts. I want the Song of Solomon. "Nothing. Absolutely nothing," she said, and hung up.

• • •

"Hello, Mary?"

"As in Magdalene?"

"No, as in 'quite contrary.' "

"Hello, Sidney. And how does *your* garden grow. It never occurred to me before, but you don't live in the suburbs, do you? I like to think of you in some horrible furnished room on the Upper West Side."

"I happen to live in a very lovely apartment. Most people think that accountants don't have any taste, but I've had a lot of friends tell me it's *very* tasteful."

"Oh no, an accountant."

"Every time I tell a girl I'm an accountant, they look at me like I was contagious. You've got to get a degree and everything, and it can be quite creative. Accountants do other things besides figure out tax deductions; there are a lot of interesting concepts involved."

"Name one."

"Depreciation. You'd probably understand that. Basically it means assigning a value to something and estimating how long it will take for it to become worthless."

Trading cruelties with her made Sidney feel on shaky ground; he had never done that with anyone before. Marveling at her ability to hurt him, he didn't yet know whether admitting to the pain of his wounds would satisfy her needs or whether it would add to them, whether she needed to hurt in order to heal or if she sought his destruction. Of course she saw herself as assaulted, and could forever plead self-defense. Sensing a tensile bond growing between them, he knew she would lose interest if he were too ready a victim.

After he had asked her rhetorically, in frustration, "What do you want from me?" he realized that she did want something other than to be rid of him. When she hung up, it seemed a perverse signal. She had exercised her power to annihilate him, to deny his existence. But she had also established that she could deny her existence to him. Let her rejoice, he thought, but I have made it possible for her to do so. Without me, her power does not exist. It seemed to him that he had given her life, and he would permit her, like an infant, to play and explore, to beat her tiny fists against his chest.

She did want something; it was clear to him, even at the beginning. He felt a powerful need in her, identical to his when she emphatically denied him—she wanted not only nothing, but *absolutely* nothing, a rejection qualified by the redundant adjective. For the moment it was enough that she needed him, even if he had to play the victim. She was right in telling him he was a perverted creep, and he loved her as his prosecutor; he would adore her for her rage, her contempt. So utterly tired of his old self, he could suffer anything to have a new identity. And if she forgot, if she unwittingly made him in his former image, he would remind her of what he wanted to become. "You know," he said, "even sex maniacs have jobs. We can't go around being sex maniacs twenty-four hours a day."

"You make it sound like a hobby," she answered. "You know what I should have done the first night? I should have said yes. The worst thing for a man who is trying to seduce you is to let him. It takes all the fun out for him."

" 'Seduce'? I thought you said I attacked you?"

"Attack, seduce—same thing."

If he could rape her, she would know that her equation was nothing more than the security of being a disembodied voice. She writhed, screamed, clawed at his naked back. Or he would just let down his pants, letting them bunch around his ankles, fettering his legs, revealing his stretch socks, and his loafers would make smudges on the counterpane. Momentarily he stopped, to refer to the positions and techniques suggested by his early studies in a manual that promised love without fear; rape was not in his index, and Sidney regretted that he had justified his nascent sexual cravings with the need for self-improvement. Somehow he would have to subdue her, and he decided the best way was by his mere towering presence, so that she would docilely permit him to bind her hands behind her with his tie, struck motionless and awed by the sight of the urgency below his belt. Of course he would have to gag her. A stretch sock would do nicely, as he changed them every day and before he went out in the evening, so she could hardly object to its being unhygienic. But that would mean he would have to take off his shoes; it was so complicated.

"I assume you've been seduced," he said, "but have you ever been attacked?"

"Sure, lots of times."

"How did it feel?"

"Divine. See, the minute I said it was great, the whole

)) 44

idea loses any meaning for you. I mean, it sounds pretty dull."

"Maybe to you, but not to me."

"Okay, say something dirty. Go ahead, say anything you want. Go ahead. If I don't react, you'll see how dumb it sounds."

"That's silly. It's got to have some kind of context."

"What do you want, Burt Bacharach? Go *ahead.*"

"Okay. Fuck."

"That's stupid. Why don't you try pee-pee?"

"All right. Fuck you."

"Well, that's a little better. It implies some kind of relationship."

"I feel like an idiot."

"See, I told you. Now, come on, try to think of the most disgusting word you can thing of."

"Cauliflower. I always hated cauliflower."

"No fair. So did I."

"Cunt."

"Men ought to realize that that doesn't sound dirty unless it describes a personality rather than anatomy. Which way did you mean it?"

"Are you one of these types that pontificate about what 'men' say, and 'men' think and 'men' feel? I bet you're one of these people who says, when you come on at some guy and he doesn't immediately ask you to go to bed with him, that he's got a problem with women. Maybe he just doesn't like you."

"All I asked you to do was to say something dirty. It's a very simple request. If you can't do that, you're a complete washout as a crank caller."

"Okay. You asked for it. Are you ready?"

"Yes."

"I love you."

"Oh, that's horrible. Jesus, you are so gaddamn sick. How could you say such a terrible thing to me."

"I . . . I was just kidding," he stammered, surprised and frightened at the effect of his declaration, and yet he reveled in the knowledge that he had accidentally matched all her insults with a simple phrase that had revealed her ultimate vulnerability. It was his own too, he realized, and he began to share her pain at the mockery he had made of his own dreams. "I'm sorry. I never said that to anyone else. I swear. Listen, I'll never say that to you again. Okay? Say it's okay."

"I'm going to hang up," she said, sounding far away. "I'm entitled to hang up."

"Yes, you're entitled," Sidney said, and waited obediently for the click.

• • •

"Hello, Maxine?"

"I don't know any Maxines. Besides, I tired of that game."

"How about Patti, Maxine and LaVerne?"

"You must be at least thirty-five."

"Thirty-eight. You sound tired."

"I had a long day."

"That's funny. I never think of you as having days."

"What do you think I do, sit here like a dummy waiting for a few moments of bliss?"

"Don't be mean to me. I hoped you would forgive me."

"For what?" she asked. "I want to ask you a question. Was that true what you said about it being the first time you ever said that to anybody?"

"Yes."

"Does that mean you never loved anybody, or that you did and didn't tell them?"

"That's another question."

"It's the second part of a two-part question. Well?"

"It means that I thought I loved somebody, but I thought I'd better not say so, and then it turned out that I didn't, so I didn't say it."

"Who was it?"

"A girl."

"I'm glad to hear it. You seem to be having a lot of firsts with me. There's something quite virginal about you. You're not a virgin, are you?"

"How many thirty-eight-year-old virgins have you met lately?"

"You didn't answer me."

"Women don't ask men questions like that."

"I've never heard anything so boring and conventional in my life. Don't be so bourgeois."

"First you tell me I'm totally freaked-out and now you're saying I'm too regular. I wish you'd make up your mind."

"Women aren't supposed to make up their minds, according to your system."

"I'm not a virgin. Are you satisfied?"

"What was she like, the girl you thought you were in love with?"

"Aren't you getting a little personal?"

"You're unbelievable."

"This reminds me of the army physical—the psychiatric part. If you really want an obscene phone call, I'll tell you about what goes on at Whitehall Street."

"You didn't tell me you were in the army."

"I wasn't. I was 1A, but I didn't hear from them after the physical. I guess they didn't need me. But this psychiatrist kept asking me personal questions without even looking at me."

"That was his job."

"But it's not yours."

"As a matter of fact, it is. I'm sort of in personnel. My boss is a vice-president and he's in charge of general hiring and firing; so I do quite a lot of interviewing and evaluating of employment applications. It's fascinating what some people put down."

"Like what?"

"Well, this girl came in for a job as a typist, so where it says *previous experience,* she puts down 'n-u-n.' I looked at her and she did have this sea-slug complexion and gold-rim glasses, and you won't believe this, a hat and gloves. I couldn't figure out whether she'd leaped over a wall or was just a bad speller with no experience and hideous taste in clothes, but either way I figured she wouldn't fit in."

"That's what I call a front-office decision."

"They keep telling me I'm overqualified for my job. I majored in psychology, you know."

"Would you hire me? I told you I don't have any previous experience."

"Maybe. You don't wear a hat and gloves to interviews, do you?"

"Only when I sleep."

"You still didn't answer my question about what she was like. Were you wearing a hat and gloves when you didn't tell her you loved her?"

"I was wearing several different things when I didn't tell her I loved her. I don't mean all at the same time —the subject didn't come up a number of times. Sometimes I had on a suit, sometimes I had on a shirt and slacks, and sometimes I didn't have on a goddamn thing."

"Watch it!"

"I didn't tell her I loved her lots of times."

"You should have told her once you didn't love her, instead of not telling her you did love her so many times."

"Thank you, Rose Franzblau. She didn't know how many times I didn't tell her I did or didn't love her. Except sometimes when I knew I wasn't telling her, she'd get this strange look, so maybe she did know after all."

"What finally happened?"

"Finally she told me she didn't love me, which didn't make that much difference, since I'd never told her I loved her, and by that time I knew I didn't. I mean, it was kind of dumb, like going up to someone on the street you'd never met and telling them you didn't love them. He wouldn't care, would he?"

"Everybody wants to be loved."

"Even Adolf Hitler?"

"Certainly. He married Eva Braun."

"Yeah, but then he shot himself."

"You're not trying to tell me he did that because he got married, are you? You'd blow your brains out too, if you'd just lost World War Two." She paused. "I don't love you; quick, what did you feel?"

"Well, nothing, really."

"I'll never love you," she said.

"But I'm not trying to make you love me."

"Then I'm going to bed," she said, hanging up.

• • •

At the first ring the next night, Myrna clamped her thumb and forefinger over her nose, picked up the receiver and in a flat, nasal voice said, "I'm sorry, the number you have reached is not in service or temporarily disconnected. The number you have reached is not in service at this time. This is a recording." Waiting a moment, she began again, "The number you have reached is not . . ." There was a click.

The telephone rang again. She picked it up and intoned, "The number you have reached is not going to take crap from a sex fiend," and then exploded with laughter.

"That was very mean. You didn't forgive me."

"Now I do. I had you going there, didn't I?"

"I thought you'd changed your number."

"Were you happy or sad?"

"Listen, don't you want my number? You might need me sometime."

"I doubt that."

"One night, the minute you answer, I'll tell you my number even before you have a chance to hang up."

"You do that and I'll really never speak to you again."

"But you'll always know the number, and then you'll have to call me sometime."

"I don't *have* to do anything. Besides, I've *got* your number, if you know what I mean."

"Suppose you got depressed? Suppose I didn't call you one night."

"That doesn't matter, because I just got some terrific news . . . I'm going to meet this fantastic guy."

"Somebody at work is fixing you up."

"Jesus Christ, Sidney, where do you get those locutions. Anybody would think you were still in high school."

"So where are you going to meet this fantastic guy?" he asked.

"How do I know?"

"So how do you know?"

"My horoscope told me."

"You mean to tell me that all this time I've been on the phone with an astrology nut. No wonder you didn't call the police. Your dream book probably told you that you were going to meet a dark stranger. I cannot believe that in this day and age there are actually people who listen to that nonsense."

" 'That nonsense' has been practiced for the last five thousand years. Do you know that Lorenzo de' Medici didn't make a move without consulting his astrologer?"

51 ((

"I'm sure he had a very good accountant. I don't see how you can reconcile all this stars-and-planets business with the Freudian wisdom you've been shoveling at me."

"There's absolutely no discrepancy between the two; even if there was, what's the difference. The trouble with you is that you're very rigid. I didn't believe in it at first, but I let myself be open to it, and you'd really be surprised how true everything was. And it turned out that all the tight-asses said it was a lot of crap, and the people I really respected, even if they actually didn't believe in it, said if it was my thing, fine."

"It's inevitable that you'll meet somebody," Sidney said.

"That's what my charts say. I bought a fabulous book the other day, and it's all there. Just wait a minute," she said, picking up a book by the clock and riffling the pages. "There's nothing mysterious about it; it's very simple. Everybody has a zodiac sign according to their month, and they've got these various influences, depending on where their moon is and the sun in terms of the position in the various constellations, and then there are these earth signs and rising signs and all that stuff. It's terribly interesting."

"You don't explain things too clearly."

"It's not something you can explain. You've got to let yourself be into it to get the full significance. What's your month?"

"May. May second."

"Gemini. But that's so perfect. Twins. An identity crisis. It's so utterly obvious. See, I told you the occult and psychoanalysis weren't mutually antagonistic."

"What's your sign?"

"Scorpio."

"You're making that up just to make me nervous."

"Listen to this; 'Scorpio women make perfect mates when they are convinced their men are faithful, loyal, completely honest, and totally satisfying in bed.' "

"Then I don't have a thing to worry about."

"That's depressing. Goodnight, Sidney."

•   •   •

Beginning to work on her project, Myrna would start by arranging the pictures she had filed in neat groups on the carpet, but as alternative sequences arose and cross references became necessary, the photographs spread out, overlapping in a disorganized collage. A group shot placed before her, taken on the occasion of her grandparents' fiftieth wedding anniversary, was a crucial document, being the most complete representation of the family, including the Englewood branch, who rarely crossed the Hudson River after making it to the suburbs. What could she possibly have been smiling about, she wondered, seeing herself sitting on the floor between two detested cousins. They were all smiling, except her grandparents; she admired them now for their wisdom.

When the phone rang, she struggled up, unsteady on cramped legs, stubbed her toe and fell on her stomach across the bed.

"Hello, Marsha?"

"Hello, Sidney. I just broke my toe. It hurts like hell."

"Rub it."

"Ow! I was sitting on the floor and when I went for the phone I caught it right on one of those stumpy legs of the bed."

"What were you doing on the floor?" he asked.

"Oh God, when my parents moved to Florida they left me with about four hundred boxes of photographs and albums, because my cheap father didn't want to pay the shipping charges, so I decided to pick some things out before I threw the rest away. I was surprised how many times I cropped up, at various ages, and I'm trying to figure out where I fit in the family saga. It's my activity program, instead of macramé."

"I don't think of your having a family."

"I wasn't immaculately conceived."

"I'm an only child," he said. "I *was* an only child."

"And now you're an only grownup. I was looking at a group picture of the family taken in nineteen forty-six, and I've got everyone figured out except one kid on the extreme left; I don't know who she is or who she belongs to."

"Maybe she's you."

"I'll have to ask my mother when I talk to her."

"I don't remember very much about my childhood. I haven't got a very good memory for things like that. Mostly I can remember the terrible things—like when I threw up in assembly or got robbed coming home from school, and the things I felt guilty about. I wasn't exactly unhappy, but I can't think of any specifically happy times either, except the ones my parents kept reminding me about. Now that I think of it, I couldn't have been that delirious when I got my first sailor suit."

"I'm more interested in your guilt," she said.

"I'm not surprised. The funny thing is that I was always much more guilty about the things my parents didn't know than for the things they were always trying to make me feel guilty about. Once I took fifty cents from my mother's purse to buy a gun with at the five-and-ten; somehow she found out about the half-dollar, but not the gun, which I then threw out the window. She gave me a big talk about how horrible it was to steal, especially from your own mother, but then I told her I'd bought candy with the money because I wasn't allowed to have guns, and then I went around feeling bad about the gun instead of the stealing."

"I can't think of a single thing I feel guilty about."

"That's impossible," he said.

"The closest thing I ever feel is that I *should* feel guilty. In my senior year in college this awful girl attached herself to me like a lamprey. At first I was pleasant, but that's where I went wrong, because she had no other friends and got to be so clinging. So one day she turns up with an equally putrid guy with black shoes and white cotton socks, and tells me they're going to get married right after graduation and would I be her bridesmaid."

"And they lived miserably ever after, you hoped."

"I was so flabbergasted, I said yes, without thinking, and even went to get fitted for one of those lavender taffeta gowns; it was going to be a one-color wedding out in Corona. P. S.: I never went. I never showed up."

"Just like that."

"I got up very early. I remember it was a muggy Saturday, and I spent the entire day shopping, and I kept thinking about her out there in Queens, wrapped up in gauze like a hit-and-run victim, wondering, 'Where is she, where *is* she?' I tell you, I've never hated anyone more in my life."

"And you didn't feel guilty."

"Theoretically yes, but actually no. I did know it was a lousy thing to do."

"Cruel."

"Okay, cruel, "she said indifferently. "But I still don't feel guilty about it. A year later, after I'd moved to Bank Street, I was at my parents' for dinner and my mother gave me a little envelope. It was a birth announcement," she said. "It was a girl." There was a silence. "I couldn't figure out whether it was supposed to be her revenge, or if she was still looking for my approval."

"What did you send as a baby present?"

"Nothing. If it was her revenge, a present wasn't indicated, and anyway, how can you approve or disapprove of somebody's having a baby? It happens, that's all; she probably had one every year from then on, but I didn't get any more cards with ribbons."

"Jesus, at least you could have sent a present."

"What do you mean? I've proved my point. Her life went on, so what I did wasn't all that contemptible. What was important was my hate, my feelings."

"Not hers."

"No. Her feelings aren't important to you either, because you don't even know her. You're upset because of what I felt, not what I did to her, because you see yourself in relation to me. At any rate, the groom showed up, or somebody did, judging from the birth announcement. You're upset because I didn't feel guilty."

"The reason is that you hated somebody because they needed you," Sidney said.

"She didn't need anything. She was getting married."

"That doesn't solve *everything*. You've heard of divorce."

"I love divorce. Divorced men are so much more interesting."

"Than what?"

"You can always tell a divorced man right off; they've got this marvelous wounded look."

"I'd have thought you liked them emotionally musclebound."

"Then I nurse them back to health, naturally."

"And the minute he has his strength back, he puts you in a hammer lock and drags you off to the altar."

"That would be lovely."

"And then when the guy says, 'If anyone knows why these two should not be joined in holy matrimony, let him speak now, or forever hold his peace,' I'd say, 'Me.' "

"What's your reason?"

"Us. This."

"You'll never tell. What does 'hold his peace' mean? It sounds dirty."

"Not p-i-e-c-e," he spelled. "It means shut up."

"Good idea. 'Night, Sidney."

•　•　•

"Hello, Mildred?"

"Hello, Sidney. I don't like Mildred at all. That's the worst one so far. My mother had eighteen thousand friends named Mildred."

"You have a very friendly mother."

"What about your mother?"

"What about her?"

"Don't get so defensive."

"I'm not defensive," he said. "She's fine. I see her quite regularly."

"People with your hang-up always have very ambivalent relationships with their mothers."

" 'People with your hang-up.' Who are you, Miss Normal of nineteen seventy-three? Look, it's not my fault I have a mother. Why do we keep having the same goddamn fight about my goddamn psyche?"

"Not 'goddamn fight'; discussion. I don't see why you can't face your problems. Besides, I'm just pointing out that you never talk about your mother."

"If I did talk about her, you'd tell me I had the same problem anyway. I never talk about a lot of things."

"Maybe *that's* your problem," she said.

"Everything is so pregnant with meaning with you."

"That was a very revealing slip you just made—'pregnant.' "

"That wasn't a slip. I said it on purpose, to give you a chance to make one of your deep, penetrating insights," he said, sighing impatiently. "You're out to get me tonight."

Whenever he felt she attacked him, he would switch the telephone receiver to the other ear. There might be more coming, Sidney thought. She wouldn't mention that he had been five minutes late calling. It was eleven thirty-five, and he knew she was displeased, because she had let the phone ring five times before picking it up. At least she had answered.

He hadn't known whether he could best endure the thought of the mess in the kitchen or her attack because of his lateness. While making coffee, he had dropped the can on the floor, scattering the grounds across the linoleum under the refrigerator. In the tiny space, it had been impossible to manipulate the broom, the end of which banged against the cabinets as he tried to sweep the granules into the dustpan, and he couldn't leave it all lying there until after he called, even though his watch told him it was time. On his hands and knees, he hurriedly began using a paper towel, and as he emptied the dustpan into the garbage, his nervous foot had slipped from the pedal, releasing the lid, scattering the coffee grounds again. He had looked at the floor helplessly, then at his watch again, and sick with anxiety, went to the bedroom, lay on the bed and dialed. The tightness in his chest increased as he counted the rings. It was going to be unpleasant. He was late, he wasn't in his pajamas, and his coffee was not next to the bed on the night table. "Who are you working on tonight, besides me?" he asked.

"Aunt Rose. I've only got three pictures of her—one in the group shot, one when she married Uncle Herman and one of them at the Grand Canyon. I don't know which is uglier: Rose, Herman or the Canyon. I've got to check the dates with my mother—she's her sister. I'm sending the pictures down to Florida at the end of the week."

"You talk about your mother and I don't give you a hard time."

"Girls are allowed to talk about their mothers."

"You're not exactly a girl. My mother used to say, 'The girls are coming over for canasta,' and they were all at least fifty."

"Okay. I'm thirty-two. Is that how old you thought? People usually say younger."

"That's about what I thought. You told me you majored in psychology in college; you must have gone in the mid-fifties, because nobody majors in psychology any more. So I figured you were eighteen in nineteen fifty-five, which would make you thirty-five, thirty-six now. Anyway, you've got a thirty-two-year-old voice."

"I've asked you about fifteen thousand times to take that handkerchief off the receiver. It's so dumb."

"Everything is in the thousands with you. You exaggerate a lot."

"All right, never mind, but it sounds like you're talking from Fairbanks or someplace."

"What about Aunt Rose?" he said.

"She was fat and looked all warm and cuddly, except that when she used to pick me up, she felt hard as a rock. As a kid I couldn't figure it out until one night I slept over at my cousin's and I caught Rose half dressed in the john. She was struggling out of one of those incredible corsets that went practically from her ankles to her neck. I never saw so many zippers in my life."

"People aren't what they seem."

"Wrong. The moral to that story is: fat ladies have egos to match. She used to call that thing her foundation, like she was a building. Poor Rose died two years ago and Herman said she wanted to be buried in her girdle. He loved her very much, and he actually tried to get the funeral parlor to do it, but they said it interfered with their procedures."

"I'm going to be cremated," Sidney announced.

"How do you know?"

"I've got it in my will."

"A will?" She laughed. "I've never heard of anyone your age having a will. We already know you don't have the other kind—as in will power. You can't have this kind either; you've got to be able to say, 'Being of sound mind and body . . .'"

"Okay, *okay.* I was making coffee and I dropped the can and tried to clean it up before I called. Satisfied?"

"Just remember, I didn't ask you for an explanation."

"You didn't have to say that. What would you think about leaving some of my organs to be transplanted?" he said, beginning to live dangerously. A nausea of fear curdled in his stomach as he waited, wondering how long she would encourage him before she drew back, accusing him, vilifying, destroying.

"It depends," she said, sounding interested in the problem. "I don't think I'd like anyone fiddling around with my body."

Nobody's asking you about your body. You—always you, he thought.

"Of course," she went on, as he had expected, following his lead, "it would depend on what organs you had in mind."

"First of all, you've got to leave an organ that is important to you, or it really doesn't count," he said. "And secondly, you've got to leave something that will take —I mean function after it's been transplanted." He knew she would pick that up.

"That immediately discounts everything in your case." she answered.

Sidney admired the way she responded to the cue. It could mean any one of a number of his bundles of nerves and muscles that she might excise as skillfully as a surgeon with her words, holding the prize aloft as the blood trickled down her upraised arm. The degree of her anger, which he knew still coiled in her, would determine the target. He waited for the incision.

"Let's start at the top and work down," she said. "They don't know how to transplant brains yet, and anyway, if you're going to be so big about leaving something for the good of mankind, I'm sure you wouldn't want anybody inheriting what you've got up there, right? Okay. Now about your heart—well, just forget it."

"All it has to do is pump blood. It can do that, at least, or I wouldn't be here talking to you. You probably think that a person's heart is actually heart-shaped, with a lace border around it too."

"The subject of your heart is too idiotic even to think about, much less talk about. I've told you a thousand times that Gemini are totally non-functioning heartwise."

"Oh Jesus, not that again," he said, trying to set up a

detour, to lead her further downward into forbidden territory. "How can you possibly believe in that garbage."

"I don't *believe* in it necessarily, only it turns out to be true. Wait a sec," she said, as he heard the receiver hit sharply against a surface. After a moment her voice returned. "Now, May second; listen to this. Are you ready? 'When Gemini encounters Scorpio,' that's me, 'during the ascendant phase of Saturn, there is an irrevocable earthly conflict between the mountain,' that's you, 'and the water,' that's me. 'Water will ultimately erode the mountain, and . . .' "

"Well, what's the rest of it?" he asked.

"Never mind; the rest is unimportant. But you can obviously see that the water, which is woman, which is heart, which is love, is the dominant earth element in relation to Gemini."

"Yeah, but suppose I got involved with a Sagittarius?"

"I don't know about Sagittarius," she said, "but I used to know a fabulous guy named Leo, and he was an Aquarius, and *that* was heaven. He had the most elegant hips I ever saw, and his . . ."

"I don't want to hear about it," Sidney said. And then he realized what she was doing. She was outflanking him. Here he was, holding out an offering, a bouquet of puckered skin and crinkled hair on a thick stem, and she was choosing to ignore it. "You're very smart."

"I know," she answered, and he could hear the triumpant smile in her voice.

"Are you ready?"

"Yes." She paused, and then, "Goodbye." Click.

● ● ●

The afternoon meeting to which Myrna's boss had been summoned was still in progress at four-thirty, and knowing he would be too exhausted to notice her absence, she decided to brave the elevator starter's jibe, "Half a day," and left early.

The Madison Avenue bus was unexpectedly crowded as she stepped on, and as she forced her way to the rear she realized that the passengers were mostly tardy women shoppers making their way home. A few well-tailored men with attaché cases got on before Fifty-seventh Street, but the smell of expensive perfume still irritated Myrna as did the touch of a cool leopard coat as she moved toward the back in the hope of finding a seat.

Caught between two women instead, and reaching for a metal loop that hung from the crossbar, she looked down at another, about her age, possibly younger, fur-clad, with an alligator bag on her lap, one gloved hand holding its mate while the other hand displayed, as if to provoke her, a wedding band and an assortment of expensive rings. Each gold and jeweled ornament, not the thrift-shop pinchbeck and paste she bought for herself, the hard, glossy handbag, the luxurious sheen of the fur, were tokens of the other's security. They were hers, without her even asking. In response to Myrna's appraisal, the seated woman smiled tentatively and covered her bare ringed hand with her glove, while Myrna unconcernedly turned her attention to the lighted shop windows that signaled her approaching stop.

The apple strudel she picked up at the local delicatessen on the walk home helped a little as she spread the pictures about her on the floor, but in spite of the self-hatred she felt at eating something so fattening, she hated herself still more for needing Sidney's call.

Getting up restlessly, she went to the night table. The latest astrological treatise from Rexall was where it had been the previous night, next to the phone, face down and open to the page from which she had been reading. She had meant to demote Sidney to the smallest speck of cosmic dust, held fast by the tensions and attractions of the celestial bodies. What was his body compared with them? Wondering if he would remember that she had not finished the sentence, she picked up the book and read it again. "Water will erode mountain . . . but water will forever be tinctured with its essence." Angrily she snapped the book shut and returned to her pictures.

What were the stars waiting for? To be part of a cosmic plan, to wait passively until orbits and ascendancies finally got into phase might take forever. Stars had time enough. She didn't. The earth sign was very promising that month, but maybe it meant death, burial, and the whole thing was a huge joke on her.

Rose's death hadn't been a joke. Once having discovered her aunt's secret long ago, she had accepted Rose's bargain: in exchange for her silence, she would be her favorite niece. Being so honored, her aunt had told her as she lay dying how much she feared death, and Myrna, remembering all those zippers, had confided how much she feared living. And now Rose's fixed-focus face, her jowls hung on the cornice of her smile, was lying on the floor, staring at the ceiling.

There were all kinds of things you had to do in a crisis. Myrna had not meant to confide in Rose or to lie about her age to Sidney. It was a secondhand lie, and she had listened anxiously while he had made his accurate calculations based on what she had told him of her curriculum vitae. Again Aunt Rose's gray face insinuated itself, and when the nurse touched Myrna's arm to tell her it was time, she looked once more into Rose's eyes, and her aunt, knowing it was the denouement, tried to tell her silently not to be afraid. If Herman had really loved her, he would have moved heaven and earth to carry out her dying wish; he'd always been such a creep.

She had not seen Aunt Rose dead, or anyone else. A medical student she had once slept with told her that the corpses laid out for dissection were none too appetizing, but she preferred to believe that like Cornish ladies in Tudor houses—or was it Tudor ladies in Cornish houses?—who died in their lovers' arms looking out the windows beyond the boxwood mazes to the edge of the cliffs, saying through parched lips something like "Is that the sea, Richard? The sea!" that she, too, would be more perfect in death than she had been in life, too beautiful to be immortalized even in the rarest Carrara. Perhaps she would be cremated too and become like Sidney, an anonymous urn of ashes, and have herself set on a coffered plinth bathed in cold starlight.

It was difficult to contemplate the stars under a city

sky, and Myrna searched for the outlines of another constellation: her family. Since Sidney, she had become interested in the relatives of whom she had no pictures, trying to imagine what they looked like from the stories she had heard about them. According to her parents, who could remember the smallest crumbs of family gossip, everybody was either "fine-looking," which meant beautiful, or "nice-looking," which meant ugly, or the person in question resembled somebody else of whom there was no extant likeness either. The face that she made up each morning never failed to elicit a negative sound or gesture, a cluck, a rueful upturn at one corner of her mouth, a resigned shrug, and on bad days, a curse on a great-aunt of whom, it was said, she was the spit and image. During her childhood her father kept telling her she was pretty, even though she knew in her pleasure and gratitude that he was lying; her mother had only managed to assure her that she looked friendly, and that was what boys really liked. When Myrna found out what boys really liked, her mother started to tell her that she could be pretty if she would fix her hair, go on a diet, have a positive outlook.

On the first ring, she picked up the phone, having set it on the rug next to her.

"Hello, Mimi?"

"Hello, Sidney."

"You sound tired."

"My boss is acting up again. Every time there's an executive meeting he has a psychotic episode. He's so paranoid about everybody being out to get him, including his wife, who he thinks is having an affair with her yoga instructor."

"At the risk of offending you, I wonder what position they use?"

"So he screams at me all morning and then takes me out to a drunken lunch because he's so guilty, and then bugs me with all his troubles. He's such a baby, always crying to me about who's getting kicked upstairs, or downstairs, and who's totally incompetent at their job —the one he'd like, naturally. I keep telling him he's got to be more aggressive, and he gets very huffy and says it's easy for me to say because I'm a woman."

"I think you're aggressive enough for the two of you."

"If that's supposed to be witty, it's not. There's nothing wrong with being aggressive, besides the fact that men seem to find it so threatening. If I were that aggressive, I'd have his job in two seconds flat; I already do half of it. I'm just not the career type."

"Are you thinking about marriage?"

"Nobody said I was thinking about marriage."

"Look, don't tell me you like being single. I'm thirty-eight and most of my friends are already married, just like your friends are, and I'm starting to get this funny feeling that they think I'm ... don't start in, I'm serious now, they think I've got some kind of terrible problem, or something. It's not just what other people think. I'm getting very tired of being by myself. I've been thinking about it. I can admit it to you; who are you going to tell?"

"Sidney," she said, "I have a depressing premonition that we're on the brink of a meaningful talk."

"It wouldn't be the worst thing in the world. What else is there between people except what they tell each other."

"I'm not sure I like you in this mood."

"I wasn't aware that you liked me at all," he said.

"I must say you are particularly strange tonight."

"I had dinner with this girl, and I had a lousy time. There's a limit to how many times you can tell the story of your life," he explained.

"Especially yours."

"My life is an open book; that's the trouble with my life."

"You had a date tonight?"

"Don't be so incredulous. I have dates once in a while. Don't you?"

"It's ridiculous thinking about a thirty-eight-year-old having dates," she said, ignoring his question.

"I don't know what else to call them. Besides, this *was* a date, right down to the goodnight kiss at the door."

"Please! Spare me the gory details. You know you don't owe me any explanations, but since you felt compelled, I think it's a bit much your being out with somebody and then running back to the phone to tell me about it."

"I didn't run anywhere; as a matter of fact, I staggered. I thought you would be pleased if I told you I had a bad time with somebody else."

"I suppose you wouldn't have told me if you'd had a good time. What's eight times eight?" she said, busy counting the pompons on her chenille bedspread and then examining her thigh to see if there were corresponding marks on her skin. There were eight rows of eight pompons each separated by a welted ridge. That made what? Sixty-four. Sidney would have known immediately, she thought, pulling at one to see how much pressure she could exert before it ripped off. "I just tore off one of those little white things from my spread."

"So you're not interested in my date."

"Did you tell her about me?"

"You didn't come up in the conversation. Have you told anyone?"

"There's nothing to tell."

"That's just the point. That's what I was trying to say. I could write what you've told me about yourself on the head of a pin."

"You didn't tell her because you were ashamed."

"You know I was tremendously guilty at first, which you loved," Sidney said, "But God knows I've done my time. Frankly, I'm getting a little tired of being kicked around for that. It would seem to me that you'd be tired of it too."

"If you weren't so kickable, maybe I'd stop. I need somebody very strong to control me."

"You mean hostile. Strength is different from hostility. Your idea of strength is finding somebody else's weakness. You have this incredible attitude toward men—they get frightened and want to be taken care of, just like you."

"Was she pretty?"

"Oh, shit."

"No, really; come on. I want to hear all about it— what she wore, what she said, what you said, what you did, what she did, how you met, if you're going to see her again, if you slept with her while you were kissing her goodnight at the door."

"Well, she had on this black dress," he began, and as he spoke, she flung her arm across her eyes, seeking to escape from the reminders that she was alone. She obliterated the view of the towel rack in the bathroom, where through the open door she could see her damp, shriveled stockings hanging, erased the lipsticks on the low bureau, the underwear of the day draped over the back of a chair. Pressing hard against her eyes with her forearm, she willed the objects into darkness and listened, not to his words, but to the muffled sound of his voice, imagining what it would be like if he were next to her, talking softly while she drifted off to sleep. "Don't you think that's depressing?" he said finally.

"It depends on the way you look at it," she replied, wondering what he was talking about. "Anyway, she sounds like a lovely girl and I hope you'll both be very happy."

"Are you crazy? How could I be happy with somebody whose total vocabulary consists of two words, 'So what?' "

"Why did you go out with her in the first place?"

"I just *told* you that. Sometimes I think you don't listen to anything I say."

"I heard every single, solitary word," she said. "It's just that I'm tired. I feel like somebody dipped me in bronze. I've got to go to sleep. Goodbye, Sidney," and slowly, as if performing the last piece of business in an elaborate ritual, she replaced the receiver. Feeling cold as metal, she let her arm drop heavily alongside the bed, thinking that she was a figure on a tomb, and the bed her coffin.

• • •

It had been a bad idea to take a nap after coming home from the office. But he had worked until seven-thirty, and the trip in the near-empty subway roaring uptown drained him of his last reserve of energy. Even the turnstile resisted him as he pushed through and headed for the stairs. The walk in the cold evening to his apartment seemed to revive him, but seeing his bed, he began considering the relative merits of immediately plunging into the work he brought home or resting first, until, eyelids fluttering, he gave up, set the alarm for eleven and fell asleep.

When the buzzer went off he groggily swung his legs to the floor so as not to wander off into sleep again. The unopened briefcase reproached him as he sat on the bed, leafing through the newspaper he had brought home. As he read the headlines, it seemed to him that his own movement in time and space was illusory; he remained fixed while events hove before him, brief mirages which shimmered and dissolved. News on a grand scale had come to remind him of his own insignificance and he no longer followed the fortunes of nations, causes and movements. He read the columns to discover bogus secrets revealed, and checked the obituaries. The back pages told him of life in the outer boroughs, outrages in dim hallways, cramped elevators and little candy stores. Sidney understood private terror in small places.

There was time for a shower, he decided, looking at

the clock next to the phone. He had hoped that their relationship would change everything for him, and it *had* been different in the very beginning. What he had dared to do had promised so much, but had like a crop in a drought year, produced a stunted growth, dwarf leaves and hard fruits. Was she as disenchanted as he, Sidney wondered, or did she delude herself, as he had once done, that theirs was the ultimate romance, a thing of the spirit, played on the smallest stage, with no scenery, costumes or props, disembodied lovers, loving without seeing, touching, smelling or tasting? One sense alone bound them together.

Being a figment of her imagination did have its advantages. For so long he had felt imprisoned by the median dullness of his appearance, feeling that there must have been something desultory and hasty about the way he had been conceived. Warts or excessive noses and bushy eyebrows were enviable in his eyes. Even the more grotesque genetic caprices of club feet or cleft palates fascinated him, and he had toyed with the idea of adding a deformity to what he had told her about himself. Occasionally, after imagining her as very beautiful, an airbrushed Playmate, he would add a disfigurement—an angry scar across her cheek, a large magenta birthmark—but usually he saw her as a female equivalent of himself, neither pretty nor ugly, middling and commonplace.

In the bathroom, small insults met him at every turn. The shower still dripped and was beginning to make brownish stains in the bathtub. The frayed towel had slipped from the rack and lay in a sodden heap over the drain. The soap had worn down to a sliver, and opening the medicine cabinet to get a new bar, he knew that one day, marked on some doomsday calendar, he was destined to run out of everything. Meanwhile the days passed, consuming his stock of necessaries: cotton swabs for his ears, deodorant, medicated shampoo. There was nothing seriously wrong with Sidney; no condition required a prescription. But when he looked at the contents of the cabinet, it seemed to him that life was a chronic disease, a syndrome of minor ailments that responded to patented antihistamines, prepacked painkillers and mild antiseptics. Standing naked in the tub, his eyes closed with the hissing water beating on his head, it seemed that like the soap, he was wearing away too.

Getting out of the relationship would be as easy as getting out of the shower, he thought. When he considered why he continued with her, he felt an old anxiety that nagged him for an explanation. Wrapping himself quickly in a dry towel, he convinced himself that he talked to her simply because he had nothing else to do. It was so simple, and Sidney found safety in simple explanations. They had irony and ambiguity enough to spare, if he let himself think about it: who was the victim now, and which one the aggressor, he wondered.

"Hello, Marcia?"

"That's a repeat."

"No. The other was M-a-r-*sh*-a. This is M-a-r-*ci*-a.

"I'm doing my love chart tonight," she said. "It's all in a new book I got; they give you all the information, and then you fill in the chart at the end. You want to hear what's going to happen to me?"

"Love—all I ever hear from you is love. You make it sound like it's something you can reach out and touch. What makes you such an expert? How many times have you been in love, anyway?"

"Millions. I fell in love on the bus today. It was only for about five minutes, because he got off at Fifty-third, but who knows what might have happened if he'd stayed on till Forty-eighth. I couldn't see his face at first because he was reading the paper, but I knew he'd be heaven from those long, thin, beautiful fingers clutching the *Wall Street Journal*. Thin and rich—what could be better? And he had on these divine Gucci shoes, polished to within an inch of their lives. I was sure he had a Filipino houseboy or something. Are you thin and rich? Don't answer that. So anyway, I was madly in love at nine-fifteen this morning, really. I'd've gone to Europe with him like a shot if he'd asked me then and there. Of course, I'd go to Europe with almost anyone who'd ask me."

"We met on a bus, technically."

"Don't be disgusting."

"So? I mean, how did this marvelous affair turn out?" he asked.

"So when we were passing Bergdorf's I saw this neat-o dress in the window that I'd wear when I went to his apartment—not-to-be-believed chic—and when I turned around again, he was on his way to the door. Something made him turn around, and in that split second, our eyes met. His eyes had this incredible expression in them."

"It was probably amazement, seeing you staring at him in a slack-jawed trance. That's what you call love?"

"What's your definition? As far as I'm concerned, it was perfection; we were spared the disappointment of having to make adjustments, and all that."

" 'And all that'? I didn't know you were so anti-'and all that.' "

"Oh, you mean marriage? I'm not anti-marriage, except that anyone I've met who's reasonably marriageable has never been terribly romantic."

"You want to meet some guy who doesn't want to get married, who gets convinced he's got to marry you in spite of all his resolutions."

"If you don't have the romantic thing in the beginning, how could you make it together through all those days, one after the other?"

"You've never been married. You don't know it's like that."

"Yeah, but I've got parents, and it was like that for them. My mother once confided to me during one of those garbled sex talks she used to give me every time I went steady with some little person in high school, when nobody was doing anything anyway, that she was glad she was pure when she'd married my father (like she had a choice about it) and that they got married because they were madly attracted to each other. It's hard to believe from the wedding pictures, even discounting the dress she wore that looked like somebody's old drapes, and my father's patent-leather hair. They weren't exactly the Beautiful People of Pelham Parkway. But even if they had this big sex thing for each other, they've still gone through life fighting about the same thing day after day—money."

"My parents used to have the same fight too, except

it was about me. I never knew exactly what it was about, because every time I heard the opening line, 'What that child needs . . .' I'd go to my room and eat little bits of cookies I'd hidden in the dresser. It gets very boring being referred to as 'that child,' especially when you get to be eighteen."

"I can just hear my mother saying, 'It's not my fault chicken costs thirty-nine cents a pound. What should I do, go out in the park and catch a pigeon?' My father used to tell me that he married my mother for her sense of humor, and he must have, because when she made some kind of crack like that, the only thing he could say was, 'Very funny, very funny.' Always twice."

"And they're still at it?"

"Chicken is eighty-nine cents a pound now, so you can imagine. When I call them in Florida, he gets on the extension and says hello to me and then says to her, 'Florence, this is costing us a fortune.' That's to make me feel guilty about the money they send me. I was perfectly content in my crappy little apartment on Bank Street until they decided to move. Then they started in with this business about a-girl-in-your-position-should-have-a-doorman; when I said that absolutely the last thing in the world I needed was a *door*-man, my mother said they couldn't in all good conscience move to their lousy condominium, whatever that is, unless I got one. So I said, 'Fine, you want a doorman, you pay for it.' So I've got a doorman, and when I told my father I had a fountain in the lobby too, he felt a little better about the money."

"I've got a great idea; tell them you're going to marry the doorman. Then your father would think he'd got his money's worth. I don't have a fountain, but I've got plastic philodendrons. Do you?"

"Certainly I've got plastic philodendrons. What kind of a girl do you think I am?"

"Is that a real question?"

"Of course not; what kind of a girl do you think I am? I once tried to get the super to let me put in real philodendrons, at my own expense, naturally, and I told him that I would personally water them . . . "

"Now I know what kind of a girl you are."

"But he told me that the building's liability insurance didn't cover that, like I was going to drown. It really depressed me, so one day I bought a philodendron at the five-and-ten, with about four leaves on it, and I went downstairs that night and stuck it right in the middle of all those phony ones. Then I had the problem of how I was going to water it, so I gave the night doorman a five, and he lets me come down once a week with a glass of water."

"That's one of the nicest things you ever told me."

"I'm a horticulturist with a heart of gold," she said.

"I wish I were a philodendron."

"Tonight I wish you were very rich. If you were, what would you buy me?"

Truncated dreams of being rich overwhelmed Sidney whenever he worked on the personal tax returns for some of the directors and chairmen of the firm's corporate clients, but while he knew the secret financial innards of these men—their tax-free municipals and capital gains, the way they squeezed through loopholes and chiseled a thousand here and there—the way they led their wealthy lives remained a mystery. Being rich meant having a duplex, but the details eluded him, apart from the staircase. And if he gave a beautiful woman a fistful of diamonds, it wasn't clear to him whether they were set as a bracelet or a pair of earrings. "I have to think about it," he replied. "How do you know I'm not rich?"

"You don't have a rich voice, and nobody named Sidney is rich."

"It just so happens that I'm so rich I've got a thing about it, and I've always been afraid that women were after me for my money, and I'm trying to find out if you're the one person in the world who would love me for myself."

"That's where you make your big mistake." After a moment, she said, "You're not serious, are you?"

"Oh, good Christ," he laughed.

"Well, it is possible, you know," she answered, sounding angry and embarrassed. "Anything can happen in this dumb life. What about that blonde who wound up marrying the Dalai Lama?"

"What about us?"

"There isn't any us. There's just you and me."

"That's the point. That's what I tried to tell you last night."

"That's not much of a point," she said in a lifeless voice.

"We've got an incredible opportunity, you and I. We've got something that nobody else has; we can say anything we want to each other and never have to settle accounts the way other people do. We don't have to make it all balance."

"But I don't love you. I'd give everything of myself

to somebody I loved, and never ask for anything back except . . . "

"Except what?" he challenged.

"Except nothing," she replied. "Except to be loved back. Anyway, who are you to be cross-examining me? I don't have to make any apologies or tell you the philosophy of my life. I'm not sure I have one. In fact, I'm sure I don't. Except there's got to be more. I want more. I *need* more," she said, her voice rising.

Sidney began to be frightened, feeling the force of her appetite suddenly unleashed, and he willing to give so little, thinking they could proceed slowly; an hors d'oeuvre of a little secret to whet the appetite, next a thin broth with a revelation or two floating on the surface, and by the time they got to the main course, their hunger would be blunted. But now he was certain that he would be devoured with the dinner, and drew back, disguising his fear in bitterness. "What makes you think there's any more," he said, "besides more tomorrows and the days after that? You want more? I guarantee there's more where that came from."

"Don't, Sidney. If that's all there was, I swear I'd kill myself. I'd put on Tchaikovsky and take a lot of pills. They say if you jump off a building, your body sounds like a watermelon dropping on the pavement. Splat!"

Though he had thought about suicide in something more than an abstract way, he had never considered the precise means; having thought about various possible exits from one life to another, he had wondered about exiting from life altogether. That didn't make him suicidal, only rational and thorough. As he weighed the merits of death accompanied by throbbing violins or the sound of rushing air, he knew that she had escaped him again, turning him from her with an irrelevancy, and he was relieved. In spite of the opportunity they offered each other, Sidney still wasn't sure he wanted to take the chance, alone or with her. His ambitions to reveal himself were thwarted by the fear of what he might come to know of himself, and by the even greater anxiety that there was nothing more to know. The dark rooms he envisioned as his mind might be illuminated, and he would find that they were bare; possibly someone had lived there once, but now there was only the smell of rodents and mildew.

The sound of her scream and her body breaking apart on the concrete reverberated in his stomach. "Not while I'm eating," he said.

"Oh, great. While I've been pouring my heart out, you've been eating. What?"

"A chocolate doughnut."

"What did you have for dinner?"

"A chocolate doughnut."

"No wonder you have such bad skin."

"I said I used to have bad skin, but it had nothing to do with what I ate. Everybody knows you get acne from impure thoughts. Wouldn't it be nice if I really wanted you?"

"That's very inconsiderate. Here I am, talking about pilling-out, and even you tell me you don't want me."

"You didn't like me when I got sexy before. If it's any consolation, I have thought about you sexually. Really I have. I think you're absolutely fantastic in bed. By the way, what kind of body do you have? Listen, before we get into this, do I have your permission?"

"That's the limit," she said. "That is *the limit.* Sidney, you may take one giant step. 'May I?' No, you may not; you may take two baby steps backward. 'May I?' Yes, you may."

"You're not going to do that to me tonight. And what is all this crap about 'even you'? Who do you think you are, using me for a punching bag every night? You're such a big authority on love; all you understand is anger. That's the only thing that makes you feel alive, not love. You can't honestly believe that I want to spend every night with you if I could actually be with somebody I cared about. You can't really think that I want to end every day like this. And I don't flatter myself that you feel any differently than I do."

"One day you'll just reach out and take me."

"How?"

"I don't know. We're hopeless, aren't we?"

"Yes. I'll talk to you tomorrow."

"Talk to you tomorrow," she answered.

•   •   •

Considering the simplicity of her life, it was remarkable to her how many keys she had, and how difficult it was to find the right ones for her apartment while holding a bag of groceries, a large handbag and a thick bunch of mail caught under her arm on the elbow of which was hooked a dripping umbrella. There were two keys for the locks on her apartment door, and one for the door to the lobby, which was supposed to be closed after eleven; she had a key to the office, in case she stayed late or had to come in on Saturday, neither of which she had ever done, and a key to the bottom drawer of her desk, which contained a few emergency Kotexes and a box of Melba toast. She also had a key to the apartment of a man she had semi-lived with the year before that she wouldn't give back and couldn't take off the key ring, in addition to four other keys, the locks for which she could no longer remember.

Once inside, she went straight to the kitchen, where she set down the soggy bag and placed the umbrella in the sink, and while unbuttoning her coat with one hand, leafed through the mail with the other. The very fact of an envelope addressed to her heightened her sense of existence, and although the familiar shapes and colors for the bills for utilities and the ones in Bloomingdale's gray and Saks Fifth Avenue beige did not promise anything for the future, they were evidence that she had been alive the previous month.

Handwritten envelopes did not necessarily mean that anything miraculous, magical or personal was therein contained. People who were out to get you to contribute to some ad hoc committee were either too poor to use an Addressograph or wanted to seduce you into at least opening the envelope before throwing it away. Rather than resenting the junk mail crammed in her letterbox, she was pleased to be on lists of desirable, potential customers for car rentals, encyclopedias, charter flights and magazines. Several times some glossy brochures about rosy futures had arrived from computerized matchmaking services; she opened the envelopes, but threw the contents away unread.

Not being a correspondent, nor having far-flung relationships in distant capitals, except for her parents in Sarasota, there was little of an extraordinary nature that could be expected from the mail. No ex-lover who had married and moved to Chicago would tell her he was separated and that he had thought of her for years as he lay beside the girl he never should have married and now that he was coming back she was the first person he had thought to write and did she still remember him with fondness, at least, even though he had been such a rat to her; no onionskin airmail communication arrived decorated with an Italian stamp and a Venetian postmark which revealed a charmingly ungrammatical and misspelled message asking whether she remembered giving her name and address to him the night he found her in the Piazza San Marco nursing a melted *granita di caffe.*

Nevertheless, her expectations persisted, as they did when she thought about Sidney. It was for him that she would eat cottage cheese and celery that night, for him she would bathe and oil her body, be as beautiful as her crowded and vaguely asymmetrical face would allow. Not him specifically, she corrected herself, but for any future, unseen, unknown lover out there. She would not allow Sidney to shake her faith in the utter hopelessness of their relationship; that thought permitted her to express to him a few isolated truths about herself. As long as she had nothing to lose, she might occasionally and deviously admit to the need for love, without acknowledging she needed it from him. How could she take the chance he offered her, no matter how hesitantly, when she knew that each revelation would bring understanding, compassion, even pity. They might laugh together, or weep—share something. Yes, she wanted that, but there would have to be so many adjustments. While her need was ever-present, the object remained forever subjunctive.

She tried hard not to think about getting married as if it were something to be seized, grasped, earned by effort, as if it were a prize. And yet, if the reward for love was only a poem or a ballad, which other lovers might croon through all time, it would be precious little comfort to her on all the weekends and weekday nights that were left.

If she had wanted to get married that badly, it would certainly have been possible with several of the twenty-three men she had slept with during the last fifteen years, which might seem like a lot of candidates to some people, but when figured on a yearly basis, was only one-point-something, which could not possibly be construed as promiscuity. The number did seem rather alarming as a subtotal. What would Sidney think about that number, she wondered in spite of herself. He was so keen on numbers. Well, she thought, as she had when she was being made love to for the second time, it hardly matters how many times it happens after the first. After all, who remembers who was the second on top of Mount Everest, or the third, and besides, once a mountain had relinquished its unassailability, it could only claim to be some degrees more difficult to climb relative to another peak.

Three proposals had materialized out of the twenty-three. Of the three, one had been a distinct possibility, but like the other two, he had *asked* her to marry him, and the question had drained the love from her like dirty water going down the sink. If only he had told her of his determination to marry her and immediately carried her off, she would probably not be hanging her wet coat on the closet door and scooping up cottage cheese from the container with the end of a celery stick.

It was comforting to know that Sidney would be waiting at the end of the evening. Resisting the idea that she was waiting too, she reassured herself by debating whether or not to pick up the telephone, and the discussion was still going on to the rhythm of the brush being pulled through her damp, snarled hair when the ringing sounded.

"Hello, Madeleine?"

"Hello, Sidney."

"You sound like you're doing something."

"Hair. It doesn't like the rain. One nice thing is that I don't always have to be put-together for you."

"I don't like to think of you lying around in curlers and an old housecoat," he said.

"My hair is cascading over my alabaster shoulders while my tawny skin shows through the black lace peignoir," she replied, smoothing out the folds of the long-sleeved flannel nightgown printed with tiny pink roses.

"You can't have alabaster shoulders and tawny skin."

"Don't be so literal."

"Listen, I've got to go out of town," he said. "We've got a big client on the Coast who's gotten into some kind of a bind, so I'm going out to see what I can do."

It meant a day out and a day back and at least a day there, she calculated. It never occurred to her that he went anywhere, or that the rhythm they had established might be broken—except when she might add syncopation for the sake of variety or as payment for one of his violations of the rules. He never told her he would have to travel; of course, she would have been understanding if he had warned her well in advance, but this seemed cruel and arbitrary, and the feeling of being victimized once more returned. "My hero," she said.

"I wanted to let you know that I wouldn't be talking to you for a week. I'm leaving tomorrow, and I'll probably have to stay over the weekend and through the middle of next week. I think I'll spend the weekend in Las Vegas; it's supposed to be great."

"You know, I heard they've just invented something fantastic."

"What?"

"Long distance." Click.

•　•　•

Sidney loved flying because the stewardesses took care of him. That their smiles were as artificial as the sauce the menu called hollandaise which clotted on the indeterminate vegetables set before him would not mitigate his satisfaction. It was wonderful to be asked if he wished anything else, and he never minded being interrupted in his count of the cotton-ball clouds piling on the horizon of the eternal subzero brightness. He would ease his seat back, plug in his earphones and nestle his head on the cool miniature pillow, cruising effortlessly until a light touch on his shoulder would announce another plastic tray.

When he had been asked whether he thought he should go to California, he had wanted to say yes, but knowing he could handle the situation by telephone with the information they could send him, he had resisted the temptation. He was a junior partner. But he needed a vacation from her, just to break the routine, he told himself, and he contented himself with the idea of telling her he was actually going. It was not entirely a lie, as he could have gone if he had wanted to.

The feeling of being a coward bothered him at first —he knew he couldn't simply tell her he needed a week by himself—but finding this position untenable, he readily agreed with himself that it was best to get what he wanted without a major confrontation. He knew he wasn't basically a liar; how many times had he told her the truth when it would have been so easy to invent something more attractive? Plenty of credit in the honesty department. After such a convincing recounting of his virtues, it was much easier to admit the lie, justifying it on the grounds that he was protecting her. The last thing in the world he wanted to do was hurt her, and if she could not understand his need for freedom, because of her own insecurities, he could protect her, would protect her without any hope of thanks. It was so lovely being selfless and knowing he was doing his duty. Meanwhile, she could go to hell while he enjoyed himself.

As Sidney made plans and thought about what it would be like going about his life as he had in the past, one aspect of his present struck him. He had stopped

dreaming. Before, hardly a day broke when he hadn't
some recollection of voices from the previous night, but
in the past weeks no sound had cut through the oblivion
of his sleep. He had begun to feel that somehow she had
taken something from him, and now he knew what it
was. Their conversations sealed his mind for the night
as surely as if she had dripped molten wax on his brain
and put her stamp on it. Instead of waking intact and
refreshed, he felt resentful of her witchery and determined to take back what he had inadvertently given
up.

Plans leaped to his mind—a beautiful face across a
candlelit table, bodies touching, sliding. But with
whom? His address book was a Book of the Dead; as he
turned the pages, there was hardly a name worthy of
resurrection. His entire social life had fallen to pieces;
that was her fault too. Well, he would see his parents
one night. Then there was that girl she had gotten so
upset about; he could survive if they went to a movie.
And if New York was so goddamn marvelous culturally,
he would get theater tickets or something. One night
he resolved to devote to office homework. Perhaps he
would go out alone and see what was happening,
maybe at one of those singles bars in the Sixties over on
Second. Who knows—perhaps he would find love and
happiness, or get himself laid.

His parents were grateful, as expected, and his movie
date continued to express her indifference to everything he said. Live culture somehow eluded him, but he
doggedly watched Channel 13 until his weighted eyelids finally closed. He did get a terrific amount of work
done, and did have a drink at a place called The Arti-

choke. Guiltily, he would often look at the telephone and reread the folders he had selected at the California tourist bureau and the booking office for Caesar's Palace in order to narrate a convincing travelogue when he supposedly returned. He debated whether he would tell her that after making fifteen consecutive passes at the craps table he had taken the girl with the smoldering eyes and the mind-boggling décolletage to his room, where, after ordering eighteen cases of imported champagne to be emptied into the bathtub by the bellhop, they had immersed themselves to make love while she laughed that the bubbles tickled her nose and her marvelous breasts.

The night before his homecoming, he had a tiny dream, an unsubstantial wraith of a dream, but a dream nevertheless, and although he couldn't remember what it was about, he felt entirely restored as he dialed her number.

"Hello, Melissa?" he said, feeling the name had a conciliatory sibilance to it even through the folded handkerchief fitted over the receiver.

"Oh, hello, Sidney."

"It's really good to be back. The Coast's not all that sensational, though Vegas was kind of interesting. I stayed at Caesar's Palace. But the trip was a drag; I worked most of the time."

"That's too bad. I mean, it's too bad you didn't have a great time, but I suppose it was mostly for business."

"It was, and I got a lot done," he said, wondering at her unexpected sympathy. "I did almost call you a couple of times, but it was eighty-thirty out there, and it didn't seem right. I think of you as the last part of the day."

"I guess so. Well, look, Sidney, I don't know how to say this. I mean, I don't want to hurt you. That's the last thing in the world I want to do—hurt you. But I've had a lot of time to think about our . . . our thing, and I think it's been a big mistake for the both of us."

"I don't understand."

"I know you don't really like me very much, and listen, I'm not all that crazy about you either. You told me yourself that I was practically the last person in the world you wanted to end up with every night."

"You know I didn't mean that. I was angry. I don't like hearing you talk this way. You sound so depressed," he said, the phrases connected by unresponsive silences.

"I've always been a believer in the idea that something was better than nothing. I'm sorry, I didn't mean it the way it sounded . . . maybe I did. Anyway, I don't think I believe it now. I've never broken off with anybody until I had somebody else."

"Is there somebody else?" Sidney asked.

"No," she said after a short pause.

"What are you trying to prove, that it's lousy being all by yourself?" He ached to tell her of his lie, but the surprise of her defenselessness so magnified his remorse that he could think of nothing else. "Now that I'm back," he said, "it doesn't seem that I ever went away."

"But you went, and I think it's all turned out for the best."

"But look at it this way. You said yourself that we weren't anything to each other, that there was just you and me, so how can you give me up when you haven't got me to *give* up."

"You've got a point—a dumb one, but a point."

"I think you're cheering up," he answered with a sense of relief that he wouldn't have to think about his lie again.

"I'm not. I'm serious. Darling, we can't go on like this," she recited in a stagey voice. "Of all the impossible relationships I've had in my life, this has got to be the most impossible. At this point in my, uh . . . life, yeah, that's the word, *life*, har-de-har-har, I've got to start getting myself organized."

"You can't organize yourself into a relationship. It's got to happen by itself."

"Sidney, the big romantic. It's not going to happen for me while I'm hanging on the phone every night. While you were away I went to this fantastic reader, who did my tarots—and she said I was in bad shape."

"I go away for a couple of days and you're back with those dream books and ouija boards. It doesn't take much to figure out that anybody who goes to one of those characters has to be in bad shape in the first place."

"You've made your attitude toward the occult sciences perfectly clear . . ."

"Occult what?"

"But the fact remains that you're a dead-end street."

"First of all, I'm not a street. And second of all, where are you going?"

"Besides out of my mind? A good question. I'm going to go on a big campaign to meet new people."

"You know what our problem is? We never do anything together. I've got an idea: what do people do at the movies?"

"I give up."

"Watch the movie, right? So if we went to the movies together we wouldn't talk to each other anyway. We'll decide to go to a movie, say an eight o'clock show, and we'll go separately, but we'll be there together. I'll know you're there and you'll know I'm there, and then afterwards we'll have time to go home, think about the movie and talk about it. Just imagine, we might even sit right next to each other."

"With my luck, we probably would," she said. "After all, there are about five hundred people in a movie theater, which is nothing compared with the whole metropolitan area. If somebody started to feel me up, I'd know it was you."

"Then you agree."

"Absolutely not. I've never heard a more horrible idea in my life. You know what decided me that we should stop all this? I realized that I was starting to think of you as a real person. I was wrong when I said that there was just you and me—no us. There is an us, and *this* is it. And I started to think about it and got scared, like this was my fate or something. I was sitting here one night while you were away, and I thought to myself, what a surprise that I ended up with you. Ended up! Jesus Christ! Can you believe it? That's when I went to have my tarots read—and you know what turned up? The Hanging Man. And the next night I was sitting here watching television and found myself making a noose out of the telephone cord. Without even thinking, you know? While Dr. Frank Field was telling me how gorgeous it was going to be I was busy making a hangman's knot. I swear I almost called the telephone company and had my number changed right then, but I thought you'd think I'd done it because you didn't call me from California, and I must admit I didn't want you to think I was that petty, although I'm pretty petty, so I waited until now to tell you what I decided."

"Don't do anything rash," Sidney said. "Suppose you did have your number changed. Do you think that would change your life?"

"I don't know, but I've got to do something."

"If you decide not to do anything, it's just as good as doing something; its the decision that's important. Let's just keep on the way we have. I haven't got anybody else either."

"What about what's-her-face, you know, the one with the big vocabulary?"

"I'm sorry I told you about that. Honestly. I'm not involved with anyone," he said, "except you."

"All I can say is, if this is your idea of involved, your life is worse than mine."

"If it makes you happier to think so, okay. You always think in terms of absolutes, like nothing is real unless it's all fire and music. You have to admit that I did give you a pretty big charge the first time I called."

"That's another thing. I'm glad you brought that up. I almost started to forget about that. I have to tell you that I don't care about that any more. You keep reminding me because you think it makes you something special. You may think it does because it was the one time you thought you were acting freely, breaking out. But you know that's not true, don't you? Anyway, freedom's just another trap. It is for you. Every time I call you a pervert or a freak, you get very insulted, but when you think about it, that's your only claim to fame. You've been on this honesty kick with me; so how do you like it? Believe me, Sidney, I'm not saying these things in anger. I'm not angry. It's just the way things are."

"People change."

"No they don't. That's just the point. That's what's so great about love. You don't change, but suddenly somebody comes along who thinks you're some kind of goddamn princess, that you're beautiful and smart and sensitive. You know that you're the same mess you were five minutes before, but then you start to think, well, maybe he's right."

"Maybe he *is* right."

"Then I'd be wrong, and I can't stand being wrong," she said, and hung up.

• • •

While she hated her life, it did not necessarily follow that she hated herself. A paradox occurred to her, but she clung to the idea that her life and her self existed as two conveniently separate phenomena; and while there was very little she would want to do about herself, there was a great deal she could do about her life without going into a long, tedious self-investigation.

For all her positive opinions and well-formed prejudices, she had refused to define for herself the form and
texture of her being. Lovers would attach the last details to her silhouette by little folding paper tabs.
Tweeds for the graduate student and basic black for the
stockbroker. A bathrobe for Sidney. Obviously he was
at the root of many evils, and at the moment the easiest
thing would be to get rid of him. Impatient with qualifi-
cations and subtleties, she wanted to make a quick,
unilateral decision that she would justify later on the
grounds that the heart was quicker than the mind.

Her relationship with Sidney seemed like an intolerable indulgence. What was she doing, tying herself up
like this, when there was serious business to do? Anything she gave to him, she decided, had to be deducted
from a quantum that ought to be saved for somebody
else.

A rage congealed in her as she asked herself why it
seemed so easy for other people. On many wan Sundays
she walked in Central Park, seeing the world paired up,
lover-shuffling, hands held, feet in step, oblivious of
everything except themselves. It was so unfair, so
selfish. She needed love more than any of them, and she
could not understand why the colossal longing, unique
in its magnitude, had not been fulfilled by its very existence.

She would become suffused with an inchoate need,
the way an infant's whole body lusts for satisfaction
without knowing precisely what it wants, nevertheless
choking with rage and frustration, feeling nothing
more than the maddening torment of need—hands
groping in fury, not knowing whether it is hunger, pain

or cold it cries out against, insensible to the memory of relief, only aware that life is the unbearable present.

The anger began to coalesce as she berated herself for being so affected by Sidney's trip; she didn't give a damn whether he called from the Coast or not, but she did realize after she had slammed down the phone that she had come to depend on his calls. It had been pleasant thinking that the relationship continued at her sufferance, that she could deny its existence at will, as easily as she had put down the receiver. Unexpectedly, in his absence, she found herself involved with him, and the rage came when she knew that there was something more to what they were than her passive allowance.

Maybe it was a good thing that he went away. It would give her time to think about herself, but this honesty thing Sidney was on was easier said than done. It was difficult to be introspective; it made her sleepy. One night she tried to keep herself awake by holding a piece of ice. Another time she attempted to think about herself while looking in the mirror, but only ended up wondering whether she should cut her hair. Holding on to a thought was like trying to collect sea treasures in a churning surf.

The price of his desertion of her would be the truth about herself, she decided, and in the beginning, only the lowest order of truths: habits—small, nasty details that would slip by unnoticed at first, and then when he finally told her that he couldn't stand her, the way she left her clothes hanging on the doorknob, the way the refrigerator stank, she would have the last laugh, knowing she had planned it that way. After he apologized for being such a martinet, she would tell him it was too late. He wanted the truth, and if he couldn't cope with it at that level, what was the point?

Destroying his feelings for her would be easy, but hers for him were another matter. Protest as she would, there were moments in the day when Sidney would flash into her consciousness; sometimes the ring of the telephone at her desk would trigger a little documentary of their curious affair, and she would hear her voice sounding expectant and tense as she spoke the formal secretarial greeting.

"Hello, Myra?"

He's getting close, she thought. "Hello, Sidney."

"What are you doing?"

"My hair again. God, you ought to see this brush."

"Mine's worse. Listen. I've made a very important decision," he declared. "We're going to meet."

"Wait a second. I'm trying to get six months' worth of hair and hairspray out of this brush with a comb that has three teeth in it," she said, attempting to give herself a moment. "Now, what was that again?"

"I said 'We're going to meet.' You know I said 'We're going to meet.' "

"You *are* joking."

"You said we couldn't go on like this, so we're going on, but not like this. It's obvious to me that we both are trying to grapple with too many loose ends, too many unknowns."

"But Sidney, that's the beauty part."

"Maybe it was at the beginning, but not any more. There's no point in being honest with each other if it doesn't lead anywhere, and you're not willing to take the chance under the present circumstances."

"I thought virtue was its own reward."

"Besides, I want to sleep with you."

"Not getting much from what's-her-name?"

"I'm simply trying to make you understand that we have come to an impasse. It's not the sleeping per se."

"Why couldn't you leave well enough alone?"

"Okay, how about a good hot fuck?"

"You've had it, kiddo. Bye-bye."

"Wait! I'm just trying to show you that we're going around in circles."

"All you've shown me is that you're exactly what I said you were—a pervert."

"It's amazing, but that word doesn't get to me any more, like it used to. If that's your opinion, fine. Let's put it this way: have you ever had a date with a real, live sex maniac before?"

"Of course I have," she said wearily. "At some point in the evening they all turn into sex maniacs, especially the ones you're not attracted to. And they're the ones who always ask why you won't sleep with them," she continued, stalling for time. His announcement had taken her by surprise and she needed an interval to gather her defenses and find a way to gain the advantage again. "Like one time I was out with this perfectly nice guy, except that he had terribly kinky hair, and I couldn't bear to have him touch me. When he started to grab me, I said 'Cool it,' and naturally he had to ask me why I wouldn't sleep with him, and what could I say? That I wouldn't let him jump on me because he had kinky hair? When you say something like that, you sound totally crazy, but the *feeling* is completely valid, you know what I mean?"

"You know I know exactly what you mean. You mean you don't want to talk about our meeting."

"You've got kinky hair."

"You're not going to get me into one of those things where I start to talk about my kinky hair, like I don't know what we're talking about, and suddenly you tell me I'm talking dirty, like you didn't know what we were talking about, and then you hang up because it's one of the rules. I know everybody's got rules, but rules are supposed to make it easier to live, not harder. When I was a kid there used to be a rule that I couldn't have more than one cookie. I never figured out why, but I must have realized that it was ridiculous, because that's why I always took half of it and hid it in my dresser drawer. Then when I was in some kind of two-cookie crisis, I could creep into my room and gorge. Of course, my big mistake was not saying 'Bullshit,' but I was a very dumb, docile child. So now I'm saying it to you, thirty years too late. Maybe it's not too late. It's really funny when you think about it, because I'm the one who's lived according to the rules, and you're the one who's supposed to be the romantic slob."

"Sidney," she said, "I'm telling you right now, *right now*, that I think the whole idea is a very bad one, really."

"That's your final decision?" he asked in mock seriousness.

"You've certainly gotten very *macho* since your trip

to the Coast. What did you do, luck into a starlet out there?"

"Yes or no?"

"I don't want to have to deal with you in the flesh."

"Is that all you've got on your mind?" he asked.

"There isn't any reason for our meeting."

"Except we would know what we looked like."

"I know what I look like," she replied.

"I wonder if you do?'

"Don't start getting philosophical on me. That's the kiss of death."

"You're just afraid to face any basic life question."

"Go ahead, ask me one basic life question."

"I can't think of one at the moment."

"Okay, I'll ask you one," she said. "Do you believe in life after thirty?"

A sigh.

"The trouble with you is that you take everything so seriously. You can't honestly believe that I've been on the phone all this time seriously considering you as the man of my dreams. I can hear myself saying 'Mother, I'd like you to meet my fiancé. This is Sidney.' And then she'd say 'Very nice, darling, but why does he have to wear that handkerchief around his mouth? It doesn't look right; what will the neighbors say?' "

"You could say I had kinky teeth."

"Why don't we forget the whole thing?" she suggested.

"We can't forget each other, even if we don't meet. Especially if we don't meet."

"You'd be amazed what I can forget if I put my mind

to it. What do you mean 'especially if we don't meet'?"

"I mean that if we don't meet, you will be left wondering about all the things you never found out about me. I'll be the only person you had a relationship with who you never met. You'll have to remember me, regardless of everything else."

"There are lots of people I've known who I didn't know anything about, and I can hardly remember them."

"You're not making any sense," he said.

"When you're in one of your famous philosphical moods, think about it, and you'll see what I mean."

"There's something else: people remember the secrets about themselves. Now, if I told anybody about us, they'd think you were very strange—I mean, they wouldn't be able to understand what actually happened. It's different from admitting that you had an affair—everybody has affairs. It's like you said about the guy with the kinky hair. You know what you're saying isn't crazy, but you'd never be able to convince him it wasn't. I know I'd never tell anyone about you."

"That's because you've got this teeny problem about guilt. It's so classic. You feel guilty, so you project your feelings onto another person and make them into these judgmental figures. That's the way you've always thought of me."

"Very pat."

"*You* can hardly afford to put down one of the basic theories of psychiatry, except, of course, if you're such a big genius that you know more than Freud."

"I'm not arguing with the concept, just the way you're using it."

"It's my fault. Why are you attacking me?"

"I'm not. I'm saying something I think is the truth, which you don't happen to like."

"For a change, I wish somebody would tell me the truth and make it pleasant."

"If we met, I'd tell you your eyes were like limpid pools."

"Oh, Sidney, would you really?" she said. "What else?"

"That your lips were like ripe fruit."

"What kind of fruit?"

"Pomegranates."

"Great. What else?"

"That your skin was like satin."

"What else?" she murmured.

"I'm not going through my whole repertoire now."

"I've got to admit that my skin isn't exactly like satin."

"Gabardine?" A silence. "Velvet."

"Yeah, velvet."

"So?"

"So I'll think about it."

"Talk to you tomorrow."

"Tomorrow."

•   •   •

"Hello, Melanie?"

"Why couldn't your name be Ashley?"

"So?"

"If your name were Ashley, I'd meet you in a second."

"What have you decided?"

"I'm still deciding."

"You don't have to sleep with me, you know; we could just have a drink."

"You're too much. One thing I have decided: you wouldn't be such a red-hot lover. It doesn't figure."

"Let's not get into that. I meant that since we've known each other for some time, it wouldn't be like you were going to bed with me on a first date, or anything like that."

"Oh God," she sighed.

"Stop making me out to be some enormous square."

"Cube."

"Okay, *okay.*"

"Suppose we met, just suppose. We'd pretend that we'd never even spoken—we'd be complete strangers. We'd never talk about anything we knew about before until after we told each other face-to-face. I'd tell you about my pictures, you'd tell me about . . . I don't know what you'd tell me about, like we'd heard it for the first time."

"That's silly."

"If we did meet, it's got to be someplace public. Not that I'm scared. I don't want to know what your apartment looks like, and I don't want you to know where I live, so when I decide to end this thing, I can still call the phone company and have my number changed."

"If that's the way you want it."

"I don't want it any way. What about this? Suppose I got all done up the first time—wig, false eyelashes, lots of make-up out to here, and then gradually I'd peel it off, depending on whether I liked you, and after about the fourth or fifth time, I'd look like I usually do. If the first time was a big, fat nothing, you'd never be able to recognize me again, though I'd probably either love you or hate you on sight."

"I don't think you would feel either," Sidney said.

"So what's the inducement? What's the point?"

"There is no point."

"Life is a blunt instrument," she said.

"The body of an unidentified woman was discovered in a vacant lot in the Bushwick section of Brooklyn early today. The coroner's report stated that the fatal wound had been inflicted by a blunt instrument. Later a police spokesman said that the body was fully clothed and there were no signs of criminal assault."

"I love it, except for the last part."

Meeting him would be a mistake, she knew. What little she had managed to save from the first moments of contact had worn very thin during the last weeks, and she struggled to maintain a holding action against complete disillusionment. If they met, no shred of fantasy would be left to her, but suddenly she realized that was precisely what she wanted. It would mean giving up the comfort of his dutiful calls, but she looked forward to being deprived of that luxury; perhaps the ensuing loneliness would this time somehow effect a change in her. Seeing him was the only solution, the only ending, and she would be free of him forever. Never before had she decided to sound the death knell for her own fantasies.

"Wait a minute," she said, and getting up from the

bed, went to the bureau and selected a bottle of scented oil, which she dripped in a thin worm on her naked arm and proceeded to massage while hugging the phone to her ear with her shoulder. "Yes! I decided yes." There was a silence. "Did you change your mind?" she asked. "You did ask me out."

"That's a pretty dramatic decision. Are you sure you've thought this thing out?"

"There is no *thing*."

"You always get angry when I express some genuine interest in your well-being."

"I'm doing this for purely selfish reasons. That ought to make you feel better."

"The question is where? Where do we meet?"

"If you say under the clock at the Biltmore, I'll scream. I never thought of it before, but there's something very *fifties* about you, Sidney."

"I don't think the generation gap is one of our problems. But since you're such a trendy swinger, why don't we meet in one of those singles bars."

"I've never been in one of those places," she said, remembering how she and her friend Sylvia had gone together one night and talked in the sweltering mob until Sylvia went off with an account executive, or so he said, from Thompson, leaving her with the scion of a hosiery manufacturer.

"Then we could go to a quiet little restaurant afterwards."

"I knew you were cheap."

"I happen to like good, unpretentious food."

"Cheap."

"We'll meet at a place called The Artichoke; it's between Sixty-second and Sixty-third on Second," he said. "Now, how will I know you?"

"Sidney," she admonished, "if you can't instantly pick me out of three thousand shrieking, hysterical secretaries, airline hostesses and dental assistants, the whole thing is positively off. Off!" Already she was up again, at the closet, pushing her dresses on their hangers along the rack, as if they were on sale.

"Just tell me what you look like."

"Suppose I said I was fabulously beautiful?"

"I'd be surprised, and I'd be very nervous."

"Suppose I said I was really ugly?"

"Has anybody ever told you that you were really ugly?"

"Not *really* ugly, just ugly."

"They must have been angry with you."

"They were," she said, grateful for his understanding.

"I'd rather make up my own mind. I have rather peculiar taste in women."

"I've got a fantastic body," she said, fearing she had admitted too much, thinking he might change his mind. "If I don't have a lunch date tomorrow, I'll see what they have at Saks. I'll tell you what I'll be wearing so you'll recognize me." she went on, thinking it more judicious than giving too precise a description of her face.

"I'm very excited about this."

"I'll talk to you tomorrow," she replied, hanging up.

· · ·

"Hello, Marjorie?"

"Hello. I wish you'd take that handkerchief off the receiver. That must have been a B-picture you saw. We'd better call it off."

"What do you mean *off*?"

"Off. You know: on-off. Off."

"Look, don't panic. We've come this far."

"You mean I've come this far."

"I know. But really, in all the time we've known each other, I think I've behaved like a perfect gentleman."

"Oh yeah, you are a paragon," she said, pausing between each word.

"You must admit I didn't turn out to be what you thought I was."

"I don't know yet."

"I've improved. You're always putting me down."

"Well, you have improved with age," she said, "but you had nowhere to go but up."

"There you go again. You didn't exactly refuse to talk to me. And don't start with that business about changing your number."

"Okay, not this time."

"Have you decided what you're going to wear?"

When he spoke of how she might look, she softened. "No. There's absolutely nothing in my closet that would be suitable for the occasion, and everything at Saks looked too old. I thought maybe something red."

"Why not white?"

"Don't be funny. I saw a great pants suit advertised in the paper the other day. They said it comes in lime, plum and persimmon. Is persimmon red? If they've got it in red, I might get it. I look good in pants."

"You ought to, if your body's as good as you say it is." He had gone over the boundary; there was a silence while she let him contemplate his transgression.

"Don't talk dirty," she said.

"Who's talking dirty? You brought it up in the first place."

"I'm not going."

"Yes you are."

"Yes I am. You're so masterful."

"When will you know about your costume?"

"It's not Halloween, you know."

"Your frock?"

"How about a freak-frock?"

"Goodbye," said Sidney.

"G'bye." She put down the receiver.

•   •   •

The bar was crowded. Swinging singles, she thought with dismay. I'm single; God knows I'm single, and so does everybody else in the joint. Shrinking back from the din, trying to press herself farther back into the corner where she sat, but still feeling the bludgeon of the noise and the cloying warmth from the fake Tiffany lampshades, she took a pair of sunglasses from her purse and put them on.

When she had bought the pants suit, Sidney had

questioned her closely for a detailed description. What kind of red was it? Did the jacket have pockets, and if so, where and how big? What about the buttons? Brass. Plain or decorated?

"What are you going to do, come over and glom my buttons? That's a new approach, even for you."

"I simply want to be sure I've got the right person."

"What are you going to wear, by the way?"

"I don't know." he answered. "It's kind of silly for me to go out and buy something special."

"You've got no sense of drama."

"Men's clothes are pretty much all the same. I thought about a red carnation in my buttonhole."

"Corny."

"At least you'll be able to recognize me. How many guys walk around with carnations in their lapels."

"I hoped you'd have at least one distinguishing mark."

"None that show."

Considering she might find out for herself soon enough, she decided to let that one go. "I did hope against hope that you'd come up with something more imaginative, like a burning brand." Then, casually, she said, "Eight-thirty, tomorrow night."

After a silence. "See you tomorrow night."

"Yeah, it looks that way," she said, hanging up.

The next night she resolved not to spend too much time on her hair and face; he could take her or leave her, as it would be the first and last time they would meet. But she did cast a hypercritical look at herself in the mirror, experimented with an expression or two (joy and despair), ran her tongue over her teeth to check for lipstick, then told herself she was an idiot, picked up her purse and left.

From the corner beyond the bar, she panned the room. Protected by the sunglasses, she did not have to conceal the anxious look, searching for the spot of red and a pair of eyes that would arrest hers in a moment of recognition. Knowing he would be prompt, she had purposely been fifteen minutes late, found a corner farthest from the decibel center of the bar, hoping to prolong his disappointment at not finding her there waiting. But it was now nine o'clock, and no red carnation, no ridiculous flower had bloomed. A nugget of rage was beginning to form within her again, and she almost moved from the place where she sat into the crush at the bar, to conceal herself, to quench the blazing emblem of her acquiescence. She drew her coat around her shoulders impatiently, then indecisively allowed it to slip off again, exposing her. The anger toward him soon turned inward at the idea that she was there at all. She knew she had been an accomplice in every moment of their relationship, and she pushed the tinted glasses up her nose.

"Hi," he said. His voice broke into her privacy, bringing back the noise and movement in the dim light. Immediately her eyes went to the lapel, knowing already, peripherally, that the red signal wasn't there. She smiled reflexively, watching him appraise her. "Is this seat taken?" he said, looking down at her, pointing to the chair and her purse on it. "Are you waiting for somebody?"

"Yes . . . well, no, not really," she answered, drawing

the coat around her shoulders. He was laughing. "What's so funny?"

"Nothing," he said as the laugh subsided. "Can I sit down? May I buy you a drink?"

He ought to let his hair grow longer around the sides and back, she thought. In his double-breasted blue blazer, she couldn't tell whether he had a flat stomach. He was at an age when abdomens had a tendency to go, and she would definitely not spend the rest of her life with a person who would turn out to have a pot; an overall tendency to thicken over the years, yes. After all, he couldn't expect *her* to remain forever a perfect size ten after two children, so she could be understanding, to a point. But they had those belts now, with weights, so anybody who cared about himself didn't have to go around looking like a pear. She thought of her rage, and decided to take a chance, nodding yes to his invitation.

"What are you drinking?" he asked.

"Martini-rocks, with a twist."

"Don't go away," he said over his shoulder as he sidestepped into the crowd toward the bar. While he was gone, she slipped her arms into the coat and knotted a silk scarf about her throat. Rings of red showed at the cuffs, and reaching inside the coat, she tugged at the sleeves. Presently the stranger returned. "I said don't go away."

"I'm still here, but I can't stay long."

"What's your name?"

"Myrna." She watched his face for the usual reaction. "Yeah, I know, it's an awful name. My mother was crazy about Myrna Loy. After I was born she wanted to get an Airedale, but my father said it was a crime to have a dog in a New York apartment. So she got this goldfish she called Asta. You know, *The Thin Man.* By the time I was four she'd gotten about a hundred goldfish named Asta, and I hated my name so much that I finally put the aquarium on the radiator and the last one boiled to death."

"Did they punish you?"

"No. They were on a big progressive kick. We had a lengthy discussion and they told me I could change my name when I was eighteen. By then it didn't seem worth it."

"My name's Jonathan." She looked at him inquiringly. "Jonathan Greene, with an 'e.' "

Myrna Greene, she thought. It could be worse. "Jonathan. That's nice. It inspires confidence. Very biblical."

"Who were you waiting for?" he asked.

Putting her hand melodramatically to her breast, she said, "My demon lover."

"Here?" he replied, looking dubiously at the press of bodies.

"Actually, I was waiting for a friend—a girl friend. She's been having a bad time with this guy and she wanted to talk to me about it, though I can't understand why she'd want to talk about it here. You can hardly hear yourself think."

"Maybe she thought she might meet somebody else and solve her problem in one fell swoop," he suggested, watching her reach for her drink. "What do you do?"

"About what?" said Myrna. He waited. "Nothing much. You see, I'm independently poor. Okay, It's just that the question is so categorizing. I'm an assistant to a vice-president."

"Is he in charge of anything besides you?"

"Not much." She laughed. "But he likes to think he is. What are you in?"

"In, or into?" Now she waited. "I'm in market research."

"I didn't know markets needed researching, except maybe the Gristede's in my neighborhood. They charged me eighteen cents for a lemon the other day."

"Are you always so critical of perfect strangers?"

"If you're perfect, I'll stop."

"Those glasses are too much," he said, laughing again. "It's pitch-dark in here."

She slid the glasses down to the end of her nose and peered over them like an old lady inspecting a dirty child. Mimicking her gesture, he leaned forward. "You win," she said, putting her glasses on the table next to a bowl of peanuts. As he reached out, she withdrew her hand.

"I wanted a nut," he said, searching the bowl for one that had the two halves still together. "I think I got one."

"Don't play with your food." It was practically like advertising, she thought, being in the bar alone: *Girl passing for thirty-two on good nights seeks alliance with any reasonably attractive male.* That's what he thought, but if she told him how she came to be sitting there, dying of the heat in that coat, he would never believe her. A faint look of amusement and superiority about him irritated her. If he was such a prince, how come he was there too, she thought, looking beyond him into the crowd, shaking her head disapprovingly to convince him this wasn't where she was usually to be found, with the cocktail napkins and stale nuts. Almost resolving to go, she revived her lovelorn friend instead. "I can't understand what happened to Sylvia."

"She's probably worked it out on her own. They're locked in each other's arms right now." He toyed with the nuts in the little plastic bowl, sorting out the halves from the whole nuts, separating those still jacketed in dark red-brown husks.

"You're very compulsive."

"You're very hostile. Are you trying to make me love you in spite of yourself?"

"No, in spite of *yourself*," she replied. "I'll have another drink."

He disappeared again into the throng. Revived by his instantaneous response to her need, she began to pull herself out of the embarrassment and aggressiveness she felt when looking at him across the table. So I'm here, she concluded; so he's here too. He's got some likely story about how he just happened to stumble in for a quick blast and a hamburger on his way home. Okay, my Sylvia equals his hamburger, so we're even, and she decided to be nice to him, to do him a favor.

He held the glass toward her, the lemon peel embedded in the glittering ice. "With a twist."

"That's a new twist," she said, reaching for the drink. "Getting what you want."

"Stick with me, baby."

"Have a nut."

As he unbuttoned his blazer to sit down, she caught sight of his flat stomach. Sold; so I'll sleep with him. She rummaged through the bowl and found a very special peanut, which she held out as a peace offering.

"That's what I was looking for. Home cooking," he said, leaning toward her on his elbows. "You probably think I'm going to tell you that I just happened to fall in here tonight, but I didn't. I was feeling very . . . I don't know, you know?"

Don't start with the feelings yet. Tell me I'm beautiful first, she thought, turning away briefly, waiting for the warmth of his look to pass. Their eyes met again as he studied her vulnerability. "That's a lousy feeling."

"So now that I'm single again, I thought I'd find out what this scene was all about."

"I'm a tourist here myself," said Myrna with a crooked smile that broke into a laugh, alive now with a rush of questions that needed answering, repaying him with a present of self-deprecation.

"Aren't you hot in that coat?"

"Dying. When did you get divorced?"

He gestured evasively. "Recently. Mental cruelty."

"Yours or hers?"

"She said it was mine."

"You're getting more interesting by the moment."

They both seemed to know it was time. "Man cannot live by lust alone," he announced. "I'm hungry; do you know how to make an egg?"

"What am I, a chicken?"

"I don't know yet."

"How do you like them?" she asked.

"On the rocks, with a twist."

"I agree with your ex-wife."

"How about coddled?"

"Not my scene."

"Hard-boiled."

"You're on," she said, standing up.

As they left the bar, the street seemed oddly quiet in spite of the sounds of traffic. She allowed herself to lean against him as he put his arm around her, the damp warmth of her body turning clammy in the cold.

Sidney, you bastard, she thought triumphantly, turning to look up at Jonathan's face. "What a relief to be out of there."

He nodded. "Do you live nearby?"

"Fairly, but I'm cold," she answered.

Releasing her, he stepped into the street and waved down a cab. Myrna wished he had given a piercing whistle through his thumb and forefinger. Once in the taxi, she lay back in the seat, closing her eyes, giving up to the warmth.

"Hey," said his voice, and she was alerted by a memory of the last weeks. "Where are we going?"

"Oh yeah, Sixty-eighth, between First and York," she said to the driver.

Once more she leaned back and watched him, poised and leaning toward her. Don't kiss me in the taxi, or you'll spoil everything. You'll crush the yards and yards of tulle my mother ironed. Not before the prom; maybe after. But she couldn't think that far in advance because she didn't know whether her parents would be waiting up, so please, please, don't kiss me in the taxi, or you'll spoil everything. But he didn't spoil anything. She never got a chance to warn him; he never asked her to the prom, and *she* had to ask Sheldon, who wouldn't dream of kissing her in the taxi or any place. What's more, her parents had taken one look at the blooming garden of his face and the rented tuxedo that fit him like a shroud, and didn't even wait up; that's how sure they were that she was safe. That's what she still couldn't forgive. And now Jonathan watched her, not kissing her in the taxi. Looking into his face, alternately grave, curious, amused, she said to herself, Sidney you bastard, you know what I'll do? I'll invite you to the wedding. Myrna smiled contentedly.

As the cab turned her corner, she said, "Second canopy on the right." The car drew up and she waited under the awning, cold again, while he fumbled the money through the driver's protective screen. There was no graceful way to do that, she allowed, as he stepped to the curb and led her into the brightness of the lobby. Once again Myrna thought that the only person in the world who knew with whom she was sleeping and the duration of any affair was the door-man, her parents' sentinel, whose sightless eyes flickered alive as they passed through toward the elevator.

Perhaps she would marry the doorman after all, and she would invite Sidney to that wedding too. Her parents would be a problem, but they would have to make the adjustment to a son-in-law named José. If they had only waited up that night, things might have turned out differently. They had gone on denying she was a woman, and she invoked that denial every time another lover was about to be added to the list, the list with which she threatened to, but never did, confront them, the proof to her mother that she was friendly, and the evidence to her father that there were other men who told her she was pretty and meant it, or at least demonstrated it by sleeping with her.

The apartment door slammed behind them as he followed her toward the kitchen, where the light had been left on. Undoing her coat, Myrna said, "Let's see what I can manufacture from the refrigerator. I don't usually keep much food around. I mean, I'm out a lot."

As she stepped into the kitchen, he took her arm. "I've changed my mind."

Trying to compose her face, Myrna turned toward him.

"Man *can* live by lust alone," he said, and she relaxed in his grip.

They undressed in the dark, and she looked at the luminous dial of the clock; it was eleven twenty-two. She took the phone off the hook and put the receiver under the pillow.

"Are you expecting a call?" he asked, stripped down to his boxer shorts and socks. She made a note to tell him that he ought to switch to jockey briefs, and always to take his shoes and socks off first. Boxer shorts and socks didn't look too sexy. He sat on the bed and pulled off his underwear.

"Not any more," she said, impatient for him. When she felt his hands and mouth, she began thinking about a small wedding with a few close friends.

Sidney knew that she would answer the phone. She would be too angry not to.

"Hello?" he said after the first ring.

"Who is this?" she asked.

"Okay. I'm sorry. I'm really sorry. I don't know what happened. I guess I couldn't go through with it. I thought maybe you would be disappointed in me."

"Who is this?" she repeated as she lay on the bed, her arm raised, cradling the phone next to her ear. "If this is an obscene phone call, I'm going to report it to the telephone company."

"It's Sidney," he said. It was the old game, and he was aware she had given considerable thought to her gambit, preparing to outflank him with bitter playfulness. "I want to apologize; I feel terrible," he said to the silence. "Let me explain."

Stretching on the bed, still unmade since the night before, Myrna reached out to touch the rumpled sheets where Jonathan had slept. "Sidney! Oh God," she exclaimed in fake surprise. "You know, I've been getting these freaky calls lately from some phone pervert. They did bother me at first, but then I got a friend of mine who's in therapy to ask her doctor about it, and he said that phone freaks are the most harmless of all deviants. He said they don't do anything else, that they're totally out of it emotionally, and all they really want is to be rejected. He said the best thing to do is to hang up."

"Don't hang up," he pleaded, determined to get her

to talk to him about the previous night. "Please," he said, trying to sound as abject as possible. "I don't know what happened. I panicked, that's it. Then I thought maybe you wouldn't come and I'd be there alone. I got as far as the door to the bar and then I panicked, bolted." Sidney paused, and knowing she wanted more, continued. "I guess you were right about me. Maybe I unconsciously rejected you before you had a chance to reject me."

"If you start to cry, I'm going to be sick. Stop making such a federal case about it. You've always made the mistake of thinking I gave a damn about this . . . relationship. I'm not mad at you. I'm not anything at you. I suppose I ought to thank you for not showing up last night."

"What do you mean," he said, quickly picking up her hint that something had happened to her.

Myrna rolled over to the other side of the bed, now lying on her stomach, thinking she could detect a ghost of Jonathan's body, a faint pungency, as her head lay on the pillow. "Well, while you were busy bolting, I met this fantastic guy. Didn't I tell you? The stars never lie."

"A fantastic guy?"

"Yeah," she breathed, "a fantastic guy," telling him it was more than a casual encounter. "You wouldn't think somebody like that would turn up in one of those places—really, Sidney, the minute I walked in there, I knew you'd be bad news. They all seem to be named after a fruit or vegetable. Why couldn't you have said the Oak Room?"

"A fantastic guy?" he said, seeming not to understand.

"I always knew you were a recording. You seem to have gotten stuck. He was total bliss."

"Total?"

"*Total,*" she said, turning over on her back. "He's terribly attractive—tall, dark, lean as a panther, gorgeous."

Still holding the phone, Sidney got up from the bed and tested whether the cord would reach to the bathroom, wanting to check his image in the medicine cabinet mirrors against what she was telling him.

"He had this thick glossy hair that curled around the nape of his neck, and nostrils that made you think of an Arabian stallion in heat. He made me quite weak when he looked at me. Total bliss."

The telephone wire wouldn't stretch to the bathroom door, but he knew his own face well enough to feel a moment of jealousy toward his rival. "Total?"

"Oh, Sidney, for Christ's sake, you sound like a parrot. Don't ask me about total, ask me about bliss. You know what bliss is. Bliss. Sex. Orgasm. A good hot fuck! Remember? I took your suggestion. It was heaven." Myrna raised her knees toward her breasts, thinking of the pleasure to which she had aspired the night before.

Sidney, you bastard, she thought again, repeating the litany she had chanted silently, rhythmically after she had coaxed her lover to life. Maybe they had drunk a little too much. Perhaps the next time. First-time sex wasn't the measure of all things, she thought indulgently. I wasn't at my best either. It could have been her fault, so preoccupied had she been with Sidney, but when Jonathan came in her she did feel a sudden release, a freedom from him, Sidney, and she wasn't faking it when she sighed and stroked his back tenderly.

"A complete stranger. You slept with a complete stranger. Just like that."

"He's not a complete stranger any more," she said. "He was so expert in bed," she added, "and yet so spontaneous."

Did she think so, Sidney thought, did she really think so? "I don't want to hear about it," he answered.

"I'm not surprised, since you couldn't even make it through the door of that lousy bar."

"I couldn't help it," he said. When he saw her, he was overwhelmed by her physical reality, not because he thought she was even pretty, but because of finally having a face to which he could attach the voice.

"That's what you said the first time you called me," she said.

"You've got every right to hate me," he answered, not caring at that moment whether she did or didn't. He knew Myrna would find a new delight in talking to him now that she thought she was no longer alone, now that she had a new lover. He had planned to keep the flower in his pocket, to watch for her, and to give himself a luxurious moment of seeing her, unobserved. He wanted to be sure that she needed him, to assert an authority he'd never had. But when he saw her, he put off fitting the flower in his lapel, to prolong the delicious revenge.

At first he had merely wanted to see what she looked like, and as he approached her, wearing the nautical-crested blue blazer he had bought, making for the orangy-red signal like a beacon, he had never felt more powerful. She said Jonathan's eyes had a strange intensity, or something like that. Then, as he sat with her, he had been on the verge of taking out the flower, and when he went to the bar, he almost placed the wilting blossom in her drink. But he knew her too well to hope that she could ever forget their beginning, and he resolved to make a new chance for himself with her. In the brawling chaos of the bar, the sounds of competing voices jostling around him, he momentarily thought of the consequences of what he was doing, and refused to let his rationality get in the way. He had a new chance, an opportunity to be yet another person; the old Sidney had reasserted itself during the last weeks, the Sidney of niceness and responsibility, and even if he presented her with a carnation-decorated martini, a romantic twist instead of a lemon peel, Myrna, with her crazed longing for romance, would soon forget the thrilling recognition scene, soon grow tired of him when he reverted to his former self.

"I don't hate you. I'm the sort of person who can only give herself to one person at a time. Love, hate, it's all the same, and now, with Jonathan—that's his name—I can see it's going to be a very big thing. I don't see that I'm going to have very much left over for anybody else, much less you."

How odd it was for him to hear her voice now, without its edge of sarcasm and defensiveness, when he hadn't actually heard it placed so comfortably in her throat the night before; he had heard her sigh after they had made love, but she had said nothing.

"I used to think about what you were really like," Myrna said, "but now that my life has become so real itself . . ." There was an inconclusive pause, and she veered off. "It was like trying to get a decent print from an underexposed negative. God, when I think of those nights with the pictures and the scrapbooks." She would keep the open box on the floor of the closet long enough to show him one night, then tie a stout piece of twine around it, as if sealing a time capsule. "Love is everything with me, Sidney, you know that, and I think this is going to be a very important relationship in my life, if not *the* most important I've ever had." She had become serious, confident and impressive, with a new solemnity in her voice. "You probably don't even understand what I'm talking about. How could you?" she asked. "How could you understand anything real and honest?"

Sitting on the bed in his accustomed place, looking at the teak furniture, gazing at the dense bars of the Venetian blinds, all deadeningly familiar, spare and unadorned, without a bibelot or souvenir added since the day he moved in, Sidney could not admit to himself that she was lying. Myrna had a tendency to exaggerate, but it was more than possible that she saw him the way she described Jonathan.

He'd had the best intentions when he pressed her to meet him; he honestly did believe that they might become closer, might even come to love each other. But the secret he possessed when he first saw her sitting in the corner, nursing a drink, watching the room through her dark glasses, was even greater than the one they shared together. Curiosity, she would say, pure curiosity, but she would know as well as he that there was more, as surely as they both knew they were doing more than passing the time together those last weeks.

125 ((

The determined struggle, the merciless negotiations for a still-unknown or unadmitted prize, the incompleted cruelties, the unexplained grotesque birth they had produced, for which neither would accept responsibility—all this he could now lay to rest. Remembering the times he had searched for a secret to share with her, he now had one that was too precious, too beautiful for portioning out. He picked the name Jonathan because it was his middle name, but couldn't think of a last name to go with it. Finally he had gone to the phone booth, opening the directory at random, and jabbed his finger blindly at an entry. It landed on Greene. "I guess this is the last time we'll be talking," he said, thinking of a way to keep Sidney alive. "I guess I always knew it would end like this."

Myrna was disappointed. Predicting that he would have a few lame excuses for not keeping their date, she had almost decided to tell him that she hadn't gone either, that she never had any intention of going. No explanations were necessary; goodbye, so long, baby. But then there was Jonathan, and how Sidney would hate him, be humiliated by her version of him. How exquisite it would be to tell him she was in love, that she was loved, that he had missed his one opportunity to see her, touch her.

Which regret was greater for her, she wondered: not seeing or touching Sidney, or not being able to have another list of negotiable demands in a physical relationship with him? In her remorseless need for victory, she only regretted that Sidney had not been moved to rage. One lover was not enough when there might be someone to make love even sweeter by telling him what he had missed, and Sidney was made for that role. She had granted him a favor, and spurning her would bring her wrath down upon his head for all eternity.

"Something can't end when it's never even begun," she said, pleased with the way she had left an opening while denying that they had existed as an entity, masking the imperative of her refusal to let him go with a denunciation, proclaiming that he would live again on the outskirts of her life. "There's only one beginning—sex. You had your chance and you muffed it. It's ironic when you think about it, but that little question you breathed into the phone that first time is what every guy has said to every girl in one way or another since the beginning of time. Except that they meant it. You're probably wondering whether I would have gone to bed with you or not."

"I'll never know now," he said.

"I would have, you know," she said, making the decision for the first time, because she hoped it would make his cowardice more unbearable, and in spite of herself she had a residual pang of curiosity about him.

"It may come as a surprise," he said, "but I do want the best for you. If you think you're going to be happy with this Jonathan, I hope it's true."

"I think it's going to be true, Sidney," she said, the portentousness returning to her voice, "and I'm not at all bitter about you. I must admit that I did think of you last night, several times, and how strange it was that you'd finally become important in my life, but for different reasons than either of us ever thought. You were an agent of fate, or some kind of weird messenger. All that seemingly meaningless time on the phone finally paid off—for me at least. There I was, in bed, feeling him inside me, and thinking of you. I know this might sound silly, but, well, couldn't we just be—friends now."

The final castration, he thought, turning the ravening pervert into a domestic animal, and she thought she was doing him such a favor. But he could afford a secret smile as he sat by the telephone, knowing that he held more of her fate in his hands than she ever guessed, the way he held the limp flower in his pocket while they rode uptown in the cab the night before, wondering if she was thinking about him as Sidney or Jonathan as her head rested on the back seat.

"I was never your enemy," he answered, seeing an opportunity to observe himself through her eyes. After all the years of waiting for the truth about himself to turn up, here it was: Super Sidney, ass-man *extraordinaire*. But even though he was enjoying a new power as her lover, and rejoicing in the secret of his masquerade, he would have to accept the part as her gelding confidant, to whom she would report the small, funny things his alter ego would do and say and think and feel.

There was nothing extraordinary about the texture of her skin, nothing special about her soft, lubricated warmth, the smell of her neck, or the tickling of her hair against his face, no new sensation except the thrill of his *incognito*, the knowledge that he had accomplished a defilement greater than anything he had imagined. It was a pity that his excitement was not specifically translated into erectile capability, but Myrna's report of his performance, while he suspected it was a bit doctored to intimidate him, was based on a kernel of truth. He had eventually become sufficiently tumescent, but the slippery frictions were only background music, like the sound of a cricket on a summer's night, to the marvelous victory of penetration; he had *had* her, and now if she went too far, if she pushed him too much, he would always be able to have the last laugh—if not, knowing her, the final word. It had been a stroke of genius not to reveal himself at the bar, he congratulated himself, and it had been very stylish to tell her that he was recently divorced. Any lie was worth the interested look she gave him. "I think you're telling me this guy was so great just to make me feel worse," he said.

"You'd like to believe that, wouldn't you?"

"I wouldn't, honestly." Sidney replied.

"You're amazing. You can't even admit to yourself that you're angry," Myrna said.

"If you're so involved with Jonathan," he answered, the name sounding strange on his lips, "you shouldn't care whether I'm angry or not."

"I'm simply pointing out how emotionally paralyzed you are."

"This is where I came in," Sidney said. "When are you going to see him again?"

"We had dinner tonight," Myrna said, thinking that she had prepared herself for the question if it was asked, but feeling a knot of anxiety in her throat. When *would* she see him again, she thought. At four that morning he had roused her from sleep to whisper that he had to go; hovering on the edge of wakefulness, she could hear his horse pawing the damp earth under her window as he rose quickly from her; snatching her lace handkerchief from the table, throwing one leg over the balcony and saluting her, he was gone. She could hear the muffled hoofbeats dying away in the fog.

Myrna had held him long enough to make a pot of coffee and to give him her telephone number. They had sat in the living room, saying next to nothing, he dressed except for his tie, she in a dark robe, wondering even then if he would call her that day, seeing him take out his billfold and slip the bit of paper into it. The smile he gave her was reassuring, and yet the dawn had come, as did noon and evening, and no word or message came for her. "At a dear little French restaurant on Fifty-sixth Street," she added, trying to give her lie the ring of truth, yet not thinking fast enough to come up with a specific name.

"Did you sleep with him again?" Sidney asked.

"That's none of your business," she replied, her renewed fear of being alone again preventing her from adding convincing detail, and thinking about how she could hedge her bet with Sidney in case the unthinkable happened.

"I assume you didn't, because if you did, he'd still be there, unless it was slam, bam, thank you, ma'am."

"You can assume anything you like. Ridicule is just another of your pathetic defense mechanisms."

"I thought that since I was the cosmic force that brought the two of you together, the least you could do would be to let me know what's happening."

"There's nothing I can do to prevent you from calling me, except I can hang up when you do, just like I'm going to do right now." Click. That was the best she could manage.

Reaching under the night table, Myrna put the telephone book on her lap and flipped through until she found the Greenes. There were sixteen Jonathans. Maybe she would be lucky the first time, but she heaved the book aside when she heard herself asking whether he was the Jonathan she had slept with the night before. It was a foolish idea anyway; men didn't like being called at this stage in an affair. She would have to wait for him to pursue her. In the meantime, she was sure Sidney would call again. Jonathan must call too, she thought. It would be so difficult to keep lying to Sidney unless she had some scrap of reality to hang it all on.

• • •

Sidney reclined on his bed after Myrna hung up, running his fingers lightly over the receiver, toying with the idea of never calling her again in either of his personae. But that would merely be cutting off his nose to spite either or both of his faces. There were splendid possibilities being Jonathan, and as Sidney he could hardly afford to deny himself the pleasure of hearing her describe him in a way that surpassed his own most impossible fantasy.

He had remained stretched on the bed watching the ceiling, as he had often done, seeing her there as if on a screen, moving her about the bedroom, the chenille spread she had picked at actually there, wrinkled, flung back across the bed revealing the blanket, pastel-colored, he remembered. In the dim light shining through the windows from the street he could see again the oddments of white wicker and disabled rattan, looking peculiarly summery as the casements shuddered against the early morning outside. She did have an okay body, he remembered, as he saw her again searching for her robe in the closet—rounded behind and narrow back, high-waisted, smallish breasts—and I got bare tit first date, he declared to himself, not believing he had really been to bed with her.

Myrna had gone to the kitchen to make coffee, and after dressing, he had waited for her, listening to the rattling cups and hardware, sitting on the couch in the living room, leafing through a magazine by the light of a small lamp, as he might in the waiting room of a doctor's office. The thought occurred to him again, the same one that had flashed before him immediately after he had come, his head sunk in the blind darkness between her neck and the pillow: he could never call her at home because she might make the connection between the two voices, even though he had always spoken to her though the filter of a handkerchief. As she came toward him carrying a tray with pot and cups, looking directly into his eyes, he became fearful that she might recognize his voice then. And so long silences separated his observation about how good coffee was after love-making, and hers about how four o'clock was her favorite hour, and his request for her number at work as well as at home.

With his bad memory for visual details, each time

Sidney went over the events in Myrna's apartment, he remembered less and less, as if he were recalling a dream. Feeling he ought to reminisce about the heavy curve of her buttocks, he nevertheless had a more vivid impression of her small back and the way her shoulder blades moved under her skin when she reached for the robe in her closet. Though he had looked at her intently, trying to take in every aspect of her face, he wondered whether he would recognize her again.

After Myrna had hung up, he put the phone down and wandered into his living room, thinking how much the layouts of the two apartments resembled each other; yet his was functional, office-like, as if making his life happen was like running a business. I'm still alone, he thought, and so is she, and the sorrow for himself and for her increased in him, the victory of his intricate deception souring into guilt, the familiar sickness. He nearly called her as Jonathan, but then chose discretion over valor, and when he telephoned her at work the next morning and heard the casual way she greeted him, when she asked him to wait while she checked her appointment book to see if she was free that evening for dinner, he knew he had made the right decision.

•　　•　　•

Two nights later he was again at the telephone.
"Hello, it's me Sidney."
"How are you, Sidney?"
"Okay."

"You don't have to ask me how I am, because I'm great."

"I figured. I called you last night, but there wasn't any answer."

"I had dinner with Jonathan." It had been a funny coincidence, his taking her to a French restaurant on Fifty-sixth Street. "And we made heavenly love afterwards." Not quite that celestial, she thought, but he had been considerate and dutiful to her, which was more than she could say for a lot of ardent men with whom she had not the least tentative flickering of rapture. Still, the second time had been better than the first, as she had predicted to herself, and the graph of her increasing pleasure soared upward into the future until it disappeared among gilded clouds. The euphoria was interrupted when her lover went to the bathroom, where, instead of hearing the acceptable flushing of the toilet, she heard water in the sink; she took the opportunity to memorize his number on the telephone next to the bed.

"Look, you might think it's easy for me to sit here and listen to you talking about this affair of yours," Sidney said, "but it isn't. I wish you wouldn't tell me about the sex part."

"You're pretty squeamish, all things considered."

"All things considered, I think it's very bad taste to talk about the sexual aspects of your relationship. And I don't think Jonathan would be too hot for the idea either."

"Jonathan doesn't know," she said, remembering that she hadn't quite forgiven him for not calling her the day after they had met. And he hadn't given her an explanation, either, which was why she had checked the nonexistent calendar when he asked her to dinner.

"I'd say that you and Jonathan had a long way to go before you could say you really loved each other."

"Your opinion is worth absolutely nothing," she replied, regretting that she betrayed herself to him, and searching for a justification. "But I'm sure if I did tell him, he would be very understanding. It's wonderful feeling so secure with somebody."

They had talked a lot about work at dinner, and Sidney waited patiently while she told him much of what he had already heard before—about her ineffectual boss, and the story about the pale girl in the hat and gloves. He improvised about market research, from what he had learned from an account his firm handled, talking about demographic profiles and media and buying trends while Myrna looked with rapt attention at him over a crock of cooling, then cold, onion soup.

"Maybe, but I wouldn't put him to the test if I were you," Sidney warned.

"I don't know why men have such an aversion to hearing about the other people you've been involved with."

"You mean your telling me about him, or him about me?"

"I mean they get hysterical if they think they have to cope with your virginity, and yet they don't want to know how you lost it."

By now Sidney knew that she spoke in irrelevant generalities whenever she wanted to avoid answering his question. "What do you talk about?" he asked.

"Oh, I don't know. Things. His work; he's very into

work. Market research. Fascinating. You can tell he's very work-oriented by his apartment. It's very sort of masculine. Of course, it could use a few touches here and there. Maybe I'll buy him some nice framed prints for his birthday. I've got to find when his birthday is, anyway, so I can cast his horoscope."

Sidney made an exasperated sound. "If this romance can't get along without the planets and stars as guidance counselors, I don't have too much to worry about."

"You! You don't have anything to worry about in any case. You know what you are? An odious comparison," she said, putting together a pastiche of human failings to describe him. "Where you're petty and mean, Jonathan shows largeness of spirit; where you're secretive, he's open and warm; you're frightened, he's strong. You're plodding and emotionally crippled," she continued, then hesitated, not being able to think of enough antonyms.

"I think you've made your point."

"You make me sound so vindictive and nasty," she replied, "and I'm not that way at all, not with him," making the pronoun sound holy, as if he were her redeemer.

There was something different in her manner toward him as Jonathan, when they sat over dinner and afterwards at his apartment—a pliancy, a need for him to like her and want her—and Sidney wondered whether her spite and cruelty would emerge as they grew more intimate. If only he could be what she wanted—a man of profligate emotions, unbridled sensuality, masterful and controlling. He did his best.

Once again in the street with her, he flagged down

a taxi, and without asking her, announced their destination, pleased to find she offered no resistance. Encouraged by her compliance, he led her directly to his bedroom, where he stripped the bed, doing a respectable *media Veronica* with the spread, when he usually folded it carefully in half, then half again and laterally in thirds before laying it on the chair. He was determined to give her pleasure, and finally accomplished his task after several times misinterpreting Myrna's Excitement Phase for her Plateau Phase. He did not usually verbalize his orgasm, but he decided that a small groan would not be out of character for Jonathan, and as he breathed the sound in her ear, he delighted in the way she gripped him, as if she thought he needed support in the crisis of his lust.

"You make it sound like you're two different people," Sidney said, indulging in his private joke.

"I don't think I could ever be as vile to Jonathan as you've made me be with you," she answered, not liking the idea of giving him the power to dictate her behavior, but not knowing how else to suggest that Jonathan might love her. She knew well enough that she had been terrible to Sidney, but it had been his fault, and she had to make him believe not only that she could love, but that she could be loved. For the first time she felt some regret at having been so merciless to him. "Okay. I was a rat to you, I sincerely admit it," she said, "but I was the one who went to that stupid bar and sat there the whole time in that red outfit, for which I paid a hundred and nineteen ninety-five. I mean, really, I think that shows that my heart was in the right place. You couldn't even go for a twenty-five-cent carnation."

"I did buy the flower," he said, "and I still have it." The withered boutonniere was still in the right-hand pocket of his blazer when they'd had dinner the previous night, but he didn't remember it. He had merely forgotten to take it out, and discovered it when he routinely went through the pockets before taking his clothes to the cleaners that morning. When he found it, his first impulse had been to throw it out, as if destroying incriminating evidence, but in spite of himself, he had an indistinct feeling of tenderness. My God, he thought, I'm getting sentimental, and instead of throwing the flower down the toilet, he put it in the wastebasket to let the maid dispose of when she came on Friday.

"Oh, Sidney, how dear of you," Myrna said. "I bet you wouldn't have kept it before you knew me."

"I never wore a flower in my lapel in my whole life, except when I was best man at my cousin's wedding."

"You know what I mean. Why can't you admit that you had a little feeling about it. It's nothing to be ashamed about. That's what I mean when I said there was such a difference between you and Jonathan. He wouldn't be afraid to reveal himself, because he is so secure in his own strength. You think every human feeling is a sign of weakness."

"You and your *feelings.*"

"Yes, my feelings. You ought to be grateful that I have feelings. If I didn't, I wouldn't be talking to you right now. There's certainly no rational reason for my having this conversation, because my life's in fantastic shape. I don't *need* this, you know."

You will if I don't call you tomorrow at work, Sidney said to himself. I'll give you a couple of days of cold turkey; that ought to bring you around. "Let me ask you one question," Sidney said. *"Has* he revealed himself—besides taking off his clothes, that is?" He expected to hear the click of the receiver.

"Sidney," she said, preparing herself for a major pronouncement, "it's not what people say, it's the feeling you get that it's meant just for you, like a gift, or something. A person can say the most trivial thing and make it sound precious." Myrna was adopting her most pedagogical tone, attempting to make him understand something she was convinced was beyond his experience. "If I had once thought that you were honestly interested in me, the thing we had together might have turned out completely differently." She could not give up the chance to make him see that she was lost to him now, that they talked now as a coda to the theme and variations, that there were no more inventions, key changes, modulations or transpositions.

"You were the one who could never get over your prejudices," Sidney countered. "You couldn't ever admit that I was a real person, because of the way I called you the first time. And you couldn't ever admit that you were excited by it. But after all, look at the way you met Jonathan. If you'd stop being so romantic for a minute, you'd see that he picked you up in a bar, that's all. Does that sound so soul-shattering? You were so worried about what you'd tell your mother about me—so what are you going to tell her about Jonathan?"

"You can make anything sound cheap and tawdry by telling the plot. You'd probably say 'What's so great about Romeo and Juliet, Daphnis and Chloe . . .'"

"Abbott and Costello."

"Go ahead, Mr. Smart, but you're miserable, and I'm happy. I'm happy!"

"I'm Sidney."

"I pity you."

"Do you?"

"Yes, yes I do," Myrna said, surprised that she meant it. "I'm busy tomorrow night," she added, "so I don't know where I'll be." Jonathan would have to call her now that she had committed herself, and when they were together the following night, she had a renewed faith in the magic of love.

•   •   •

Once more the box of photographs lay on the floor of Myrna's bedroom, and she was working with unusual concentration, sorting out the summer at Rockaway. The Brownie camera had been one of the memorable things that August, and she remembered the almost daily trips to the drugstore with rolls of exposed film, and the suspense of wondering whether the yellow envelopes she came to collect contained anything except sandaled feet and light-struck silhouettes. Unfortunately, there had been a great deal of company during those hot, humid weeks, and she swore at herself for having been such a diligent chronicler of the family's visitors.

Myrna had decided to finish her work, as insurance, and was aiming at an unstated deadline.

So far they had seen each other on alternating nights, which was a good sign, but he hadn't explained what he did on the nights in between. That was a bad sign, and yet she was glad to have the time to finish the project and to be able to talk with Sidney. The reports she gave him were a way of giving definite shape to her reveries.

When the phone rang she picked up the receiver and said, "Wait a sec, I want to move over here to the floor."

Sidney heard the sounds and followed her from the edge of the bed next to the white wicker night table, wondering whether she was near the closet or the bureau. It was exactly eleven-thirty, but he felt that she had no right to take him so for granted that she would not even say "Hello." Not even a greeting; shit, even his mother said "Hello," and he had been calling her regularly for years now.

"You know, I used to wear rubber beach shoes when I was eleven," she said.

"Oh, the pictures," Sidney said, despising himself for knowing what she was doing and what she meant, and for letting her know that he understood.

"That was a very big summer. They gave me my first camera, and I got my first period. They all thought I was a genius for getting it so early."

"A child prodigy," he said, the hatred settling inside him as if he had eaten concrete. He didn't want to hear about it, not as Sidney. Perhaps as Jonathan, later, much later, but not as either at this moment, and he struggled to control the volcanic rage that the knowledge of a simple biological fact could unleash in him.

The uncanny knack she had of reminding him of long-forgotten humiliations still amazed him. Shortly after he had graduated from college and was working at his first job, feeling very much a man among men in spite of still living at home, he met a girl he had known in high school. At the lunch counter where they saw each other by accident, they had talked of erstwhile classmates whose whereabouts and activities they knew and didn't know. In school Sidney had been no exception to her rule never to go out with anyone her own age, but his salary and his Brooks Brothers-type suit emboldened him to ask her to dine with him that very night. He remembered later that she looked surprised before she accepted his invitation. Later, when they talked in the Hungarian place in the Village—or rather she talked—about her fiancé who would be graduating from law school in a few months, he had sat there, stunned with embarrassment and fury in the realization that she had never, and would never, think of him as a man, that the idea that he might want to kiss her or fondle her had never occurred to her, and that she was using him to pass the time; he was merely an old pal, gray flannel and cordovans notwithstanding. He had smiled obediently as she told him of her intended, and abandoned his plans for the rest of the evening.

"You may think it's funny," Myrna said, "but it's a very important moment in a woman's life."

"I take your word for it." Everything he said sounded like an admission of defeat, and even with the success he was having with her, he felt at this moment that she was winning on both fronts. "Did you have a good time last night?"

"We had a marvelous time. Marvelous," she repeated. The tears had brimmed in her eyes when Jonathan told her how his mother had died when he was only seven. She might have noticed, he went on, how bare his apartment was; it was because he was afraid of becoming attached to things, lest they be taken away. It was thrilling to know he could be afraid. Reaching out to touch his hand, to let him know she would always be there, she looked silently into his face, that ordinary face; yes, it was ordinary, she told herself, but it didn't matter now, that face she saw so attractively scarred with tragedy, subtle creases of sadness about his eyes that others might not see.

Pressing his advantage, Sidney decided it would be advisable to bring up Jonathan's ex-wife. She had been such a thing-person, he told Myrna, when what ultimately mattered was what went on between two people. The words had been taken right out of her mouth, she had replied. But he didn't want to talk about his ex-wife. That was all in the past, and besides, he didn't think it was a good idea to talk about somebody you'd been married to.

Myrna wasn't so sure of that. It might be good for him to get it all out, she suggested, aching to know more, to know what he wanted from her, how she ought to be with him, willing to undergo any transformation on his account, provided he would give her a sign that they had a future.

Sidney had watched her eating the cannelloni, still hungry for information, and remarked that it was still too early to tell, but he thought he wouldn't mind getting married again at some point. It was the getting divorced that was so unpleasant.

"His ex-wife was a perfect bitch," Myrna now said into the phone. "You should hear the things she did to him."

"You didn't tell me he was married before."

"Oh, yeah. It makes him so attractive."

"Well, what about the things he did to her?" Not waiting for her reply, he went on. "Isn't there some theory about people marrying the same person over and over again? That puts you in an awkward position. If he falls in love with you and marries you, then you're just as bad as his first wife; if you're the sweet, dear, gentle, loving person you say you are, you don't have a prayer."

"I hate to disappoint you, but that theory doesn't apply in this case," she said, "because he's had some very important insights about the whole relationship. He told me all about it, and it's obvious that he wouldn't make the same mistake twice. You're just being nasty because I'm in love and you're not."

"That's true, I'm not. I wish you wouldn't remind me of it, because God knows I think about it often enough." More often than you think, he said to himself. When they were together, he noticed her high color, the air of expectancy about her, compared with his own cool wariness. Probably she thought his reserve had something to do with his recent divorce, but he had to be so careful not to repeat anything he told her on the phone, to keep straight the past he was putting together piecemeal each time he saw her. The lies were not planned; they evolved out of their talk, from his sense of what he felt would excite her, and that day he had bought a little spiral notebook into which he began jotting the details he wanted to remember. As he was creating himself, he envied Myrna's ability to suspend her belief in her own imperfections. "Ever since you met Jonathan, I've been getting very depressed," he said.

"You haven't thought about suicide?"

Everything has to be such a melodrama, he thought. "Not exactly."

"What is that supposed to mean?" Myrna asked with annoyance. She was only playing the part he had cast her in; she didn't want him to suicide on her, only to indulge her with a little exaggeration. If he cared about her, that would be the least he could do.

"I had a terrible headache when I got home from the office this evening, and I went to the medicine cabinet to get a couple of aspirin, and when I saw the bottle, I said to myself, 'What if they were sleeping pills?' "

"That's not thinking about suicide; that's just being suicidal. There's a big difference. I've been suicidal lots of times."

"I've got to tell you that I feel lousy before you get interested in me. I'm genuinely interested in what's going on between you and Jonathan."

"Are you switching from obscene phone calls to voyeurism?"

"You must be having a great time, considering how abusive you are tonight."

"Have you really been depressed?"

"Yes, especially on the nights when you go out with him," he replied, wishing he could share the joke with her. Then he thought of a better one. "Look, I want to ask you a big favor."

"What," she answered defensively.

"I know it's a lot to ask, but I've been so depressed

—couldn't I call you tomorrow night? It would mean a great deal to me."

"Sidney," she said, as if beginning to reason with a demanding child, "you know I'm going out with Jonathan tomorrow night."

"But I'll be so depressed. I bet if I took a whole bottle of aspirin, I could get pretty sick. I'd leave a suicide note with your number as next-of-kin."

"If you can joke about it, you can't be *that* depressed."

"If I don't joke about it, I'd really crack up. I mean it. Why couldn't you go back to your place? All you'd have to do is say 'Hello.' That's all I'd need. Just the sound of your voice. You could say it was the wrong number or something."

"Sidney, you've got to realize that you're a peripheral person in my life now," she said. Now? She heard the word, too, as it reverberated in the silence, wishing she could snatch it back. "I've got something very beautiful going for me, and I can't stop to think about you. I know it sounds very brutal, but that's it."

The only way he could get her even to consider his request, Sidney thought, was to accept his subsidiary role, to make her forget she had let slip that once he had meant something else to her. "I understand how you feel." Feel: it was the key that would unlock any door.

"Have you really been feeling *that* depressed?" she asked.

Perhaps she was right about feelings. If his depression could move her to ask about the degree and quality of his emotion, perhaps his other feelings would move her, or others, to respond to him. "I have been *that* depressed," he admitted, not knowing what she meant.

"Well, I just don't know where I'll be tomorrow night. Jonathan hasn't told me where we're having dinner, and we'll probably go to his place after, so I don't know whether I'll even be here. There's nothing I can do to prevent you from calling, but we usually have very long dinners. I'm not being mean now, but you do know how much you can have to talk about and not realize how late it is. Anyway, if you're really *that* depressed, I guess you can call. Mind you, I don't guarantee that I'll pick up the phone even if I'm here, and besides that, it might be off the hook anyway."

"Which means if you get too horny, you won't give a shit how I feel."

"You always sound so tense when you try to say something even vaguely dirty. But since you put it that way, the answer is yes."

Knowing he shouldn't have tested her that way, he backed off. "I'm very upset. I'll try not to call, honestly I will."

A compromise would be appropriate, Myrna thought. "If I'm here, and I can't guarantee that I will be," she said, "I won't leave the phone off the hook. Okay?"

"I appreciate that."

"Goodnight, Sidney."

• • •

"Hello, its me Sidney."

"I simply couldn't be there; I hope you understand, but we ended up at Jonathan's place. It was what he wanted." If the decision had been out of her hands, preordained, she was neither guilty nor blameless. "When he says we're going to do something, we do it. He's very positive that way."

Until the last moment, Sidney played a game with himself, first choosing to tell her that he had called the previous evening, then that he had not. Hearing her tell him that she had not been a party to the decision, he decided his triumph was sweet enough, and he let her know that he had needed her. "I did call you, and even though I didn't get an answer, I felt a lot better."

It was remarkable how little Sidney needed, she thought, consoling herself. First he wanted to talk to me, and now he's satisfied with the ringing alone. Gratified to know the extent of his unhappiness, but nevertheless determined to reconstruct the barricade to her other life, she said, "I'm glad, but I wouldn't want it to become a habit. I think you ought to find something interesting and constructive to do on the nights I'm out." She did a half sit-up to tuck the hem of her robe around her ankles, and a captive breath escaped her as she fell back on the pillows.

"What's the matter? You sound tired."

"I am. My boss went on one of his rampages today." Even Myrna's vice-president, who usually was so self-

)) 148

involved, had noticed the grim lines bracketing her mouth, and had asked her if anything was wrong.

"Everybody has days like that," Sidney assured her.

When Jonathan had called her at the office the day before, he had told her that he would have to work late that evening, and that he wouldn't pick her up at her apartment until eight-thirty. Previously, he had come an hour earlier, and the time between her coming home and his arrival would be filled with leisurely ablutions, washing her hair, a thorough inspection of her body, a little flowery unguent here, a bit of spray there, assured that in a short time she would be snugly ensconced, like a cat by a warm hearth, in a midtown restaurant opposite him.

During the extra waiting at home, Myrna began to feel restless and uneasy, as thoughts of Sidney interrupted her usual expectations about Jonathan, as if someone in the next apartment were playing the radio too loudly. Washing the doors of the kitchen cabinets helped somewhat, as did making a grocery list, but until Jonathan came, she was not able to distract herself from the question of whether Sidney would call her. In spite of the encouraging reports she gave Sidney about the progress of her affair, and her need to believe in the reported version, she was not sure that Jonathan was sufficiently beguiled; she began to wonder when they would start seeing each other every night. Suppose they went on as they did, on an every-other-night basis, she thought. Then he would have to tell her what he did on the off-nights. And what about the weekends, she wondered, and legal holidays.

Myrna knew she was rushing things, but as long as

she could keep herself in check when she was with him, she had every right to contemplate the problem on her own. Why not ask Sidney? Aside from everything else, he was a man, she reasoned, and again she wondered whether she would be home later that night, and if so, whether he would call her. It might be a good idea to talk to him for a minute or two, in the bedroom, where Jonathan, who she would make sure was in earshot, might overhear her say his name through the half-opened door. But it hadn't worked out that way, she thought, interrupted in the scene she had not been able to act out, aware that Sidney was telling her something. "What?"

"I was telling you that I didn't have such a good day myself."

"What happened?"

"I just told you. Where are you tonight?"

"You brought up a very good question," she said, relieved to be able to think of something other than the exertions of the night before. It had been nine o'clock before they had arrived at the restaurant; that they had gone all the way to the Village for paella seemed part of a diabolical plot, or a dire omen, since by now she had resolved to be home when Sidney called. "Let's say you were going out with this guy, and saw each other every other night."

"I can't guess who you're referring to."

"And he never tells you what he does on the nights he doesn't see you."

"What do you think he does? It's probably much more interesting than what he is really doing. Actually,

I'm much more interested in what you did last night," said Sidney, eager to hear her report.

He had purposely called for her at an unusually late hour, and as they rode down to the Spanish restaurant on MacDougal Street, he had explained in great detail about a research study they were doing for a perfume company. Over drinks Myrna had discoursed with equal thoroughness about her theories of smell as it affected romantic reactions, remembering which parts of her she had deodorized and which she had scented.

Since she had appeared so interested in his work, Jonathan decided to tell her that he had the whole campaign mapped out, and that he thought she might like to see the presentation, which was at his apartment. If she said yes, he would have taken her there, become overwhelmed by a sexual paroxysm which he knew would interest her more, and would have been content to say on the following night when he spoke to her as Sidney that he had taken her advice and had been out and doing, knowing she would be disappointed that his depression had been so slight that not only had he not called, but he had been able to enjoy himself without her.

"Last night?" she said. "Well, the usual." As she looked back on the evening there had been nothing extraordinary, except that time had moved so quickly, and they so slowly. It had been interesting to hear about his work, but if he had talked about himself, she might have been able to forget about Sidney—would he call or not? She had to know. "He thought my idea about the prints was great—and I said we could go to some galleries one Saturday. That's why we went to his apartment, so that we could figure out where they should go." Which sounded more intimate than discussing a market-research study.

Sidney wondered why Myrna hadn't mentioned the prints to him. Never having been able to make up his mind about what to put on the walls, he would have been happy to take her suggestion about anything she would recommend. "So what did you decide?" he asked.

Sipping their coffee, she had asked Jonathan the time, and when he had said ten-thirty he watched her reach unconsciously for her purse, as if to go. When he nonchalantly ordered two brandies, stalling for time, knowing she liked him to make these small decisions for her, Myrna mentioned to him that the restaurant looked rather empty and perhaps they wanted to close. Explaining that the Spanish brandy they served was one of his favorites, and one of the reasons he liked the place so much, he saw her eyes narrow with tension; she turned the face of her watch so that she could see it out of the corner of her eye.

"We decided to decide some other time," she said.

"You mean you went to bed instead."

"You're the one who told me it was unseemly to talk about sex." By the time she got home, sex was the last thing on her mind, feeling as if she had swum through a river of molasses. It was close to eleven by the time they left the restaurant, and after she suggested that they go to her apartment rather than his, without agreeing or disagreeing, Jonathan remarked on the beauty of the night, taking her arm for a bit of a walk.

Instead of feeling relaxed from the half bottle of wine she had drunk, Myrna felt herself slipping, with each passing moment, into reveries about Sidney and whether he would call.

Having Jonathan across the table, with that curious intensity in his eyes, so unexpected in his ordinary face, had given her the momentary security that he was hers, and that the moment of possession would last forever. But she wasn't sure of Sidney. It wasn't a question of not being able to give Sidney up; she had never even had him, she repeated to herself. But the moment of security with Jonathan passed as quickly as it had come, and as he turned to get the waiter, the beautiful forever that she had been so sure of became as ephemeral as the candlelight she saw reflected in his eyes. Perhaps he saw the same glow in hers. Did he want it to be an eternal flame or just a dripless candle? She wasn't sure of Jonathan either, and wouldn't be until they were married.

It wasn't a question of testing whether Sidney needed her, Myrna told herself, but rather the healthy instinct of self-preservation. Jonathan wouldn't even tell her what he did when he wasn't with her; therefore, she would burn no bridges, however rickety, until the flame of his love burned brighter. Besides, she thought irritably, I'm too old for walking in the Village with all these groupies. Could she really be afraid, she thought, holding tighter to Jonathan's arm, afraid now, with him, unwilling to admit to him what she felt. Not yet, she told herself—no fears until later, not hers, regardless of how intriguing she found his. No anxieties, tensions, conflicts. Keep it light, gay, romantic, goddamn it. And yet when she looked up at him as they walked, noticing a lighted clock in the window of a drugstore—eleven-three—he was little more than a stranger to her. Four times. I've been out with him four times.

"You said you were more interested in what we did," she said to Sidney.

"I guess I'm ambivalent," he said.

After they had walked a few blocks, Myrna had told him as gently as she could that she just couldn't go to his place tonight, even though she was anxious to see what his report looked like. Squeezing his arm, laughing away the furrows above her nose, she pointed out that once they got home she wouldn't get back to her apartment, and that there was an office joke that if somebody showed up at work in the same dress, it meant that they had slept out, and that the last time she had spent the night at his house, she had been able to get home and change, but tomorrow she had an early appointment and she didn't want to go staggering around the streets at seven to get to her house in time to get into another dress. Besides which, she was cold and couldn't they take a cab right away.

Sidney watched her relief as they headed uptown, and she was so nearly her usual self by the time they reached her neighborhood that he checked his watch. He announced it was eleven-twenty as they approached Sixty-eighth Street, and asked the driver to stop at the nearest open deli, as he wanted to get something for breakfast, telling her, reluctantly and with embarrassment, that one of his things was a mandatory glass of apricot nectar in the morning. She might as well find out the worst about him right then and there, he said. Myrna was having a little trouble laughing by this time, he noticed.

Though it was too late by the time they had reached the door of her apartment, Myrna had her key ready, inserted it into the keyhole like a stiletto and burst into the apartment as if she wanted to surprise an intruder. Jonathan asked her if she was all right after she stood listening intently in the mocking silence, the light from the kitchen in the otherwise dark apartment raking her troubled face. You couldn't even feel safe in your own apartment in this crazy city, she heard herself mumbling, remembering the first time Sidney had called.

The dread that had shook her in the street held her again, and she involuntarily took a step toward Jonathan, trying to escape its hold. When she felt the rough tweed of his coat against her cheek, she almost said his name, but quickly recovered, and looking again into his eyes, began wondering what he did on the nights he wasn't with her.

"You didn't answer my question about this guy who doesn't tell about what he does when he doesn't see this girl," Myrna said to Sidney.

"I guess it depends on the way they feel about each other."

"Of course it depends on the way they feel about each other. They adore each other, that's the way they feel. She'd really like to call him up on one of their off nights, to see if he's there, but she doesn't, because men get very clutchy if you call them, like you're invading their privacy."

"I think that's a wise decision."

"It's not a decision," she said. If he was not there, she

could only conclude that he was **out** with somebody else, but while the idea of competing for him enhanced his attractiveness, her rival would be prettier and more clever than she, and Jonathan would be so carried away that not only would he be silent about his ex-wife, he would forget that he had even been married before. "It's simply the way you have to play the game."

"She ought to come right out and ask him point-blank. What has she got to lose?" Sidney asked. "Some people might think the question was a little out of line, but only she would be able to judge whether he'd feel that way. The question seems to me whether she really wants to know what he does, or whether she's only upset because he won't tell her."

"What's this business about 'won't'? You make it sound like he's deliberately tormenting her. You would think that way."

"Look at it this way: either she can figure that he wants to see her every other night, or that he *doesn't* want to see her every other night. It depends on whether she's an optimist or a pessimist."

Why did it have to depend on anything, Myrna wondered. Why couldn't it be simple? According to the way she understood falling bodies, they obeyed one law: gravity. Why couldn't falling in love be the same? "You're a big help."

"If I were in her situation, I wouldn't ask him."

"She is not in a 'situation,' " she replied, thinking that her parents would have called it a position, remembering the doorman who stirred from his trance the night before as she rushed through the lobby to the elevator. "Oh Christ, I'm sorry I brought the whole thing up."

As they talked, Myrna recalled how she had asked the unstated question of Jonathan, drawing away from him in the hall, confronting his eyes again. How perfect it would have been if he had answered, having read her mind and understood her look without her having to say anything. That was the language of love; had he known what the look cost her, he would not have demanded by his silence that she ask the question.

By all rights, she thought, she ought to be furious with Sidney. It was he who had curled up in her, an incubus, waiting until her resistance was lowered. But she couldn't blame him, likening him to an infection, which was simply trying to be what it was. You couldn't blame a virus for making you sick. All it wanted to do was find a nice, wet, warm, dark place to settle down, to multiply, and the sickness was beside the point as far as the virus was concerned. Jonathan would be her medicine, and she would have to find a way of increasing the dosage. "I'm tired," she said.

"Of what?"

"Of being tired of being tired of being tired," Myrna replied, her voice becoming lost. "I've got to go to sleep. I think I'm coming down with something." She was beginning to remember the previous evening in reverse, starting by seeing herself sitting limply on her couch and walking stiffly backwards toward the door, like the cartoons her father used to show at birthday parties, threaded into the projector upside down and backwards, which used to be funny when shown in regular sequence but were positively riotous when put the wrong way in.

"It's me."

"Hello, Sidney."

When the phone rang, Myrna had just finished cleaning up the debris of the night before, putting off doing it not out of distaste for housework, but because the greasy dishes and sticky glasses in the kitchen reminded her that Jonathan had been there. Two coffee cups still stood on the table where, after spending the night, he had sat with her, fresh from the shower, clean-shaven, having used her leg razor. Myrna had put the cups with the other dishes in the sink, but she couldn't yet bring herself to move the razor, which lay where he had left it on the bathroom shelf instead of the corner of the tub, as if it was the room in which Jonathan had died and she had vowed to keep it as it was, always.

"How's your cold?" Sidney asked.

"It was a false alarm. You were absolutely wrong. I just want you to know that I asked Jonathan what he did when he wasn't with me, and he gave me a perfectly straightforward answer."

The chicken Myrna had made for him had been delicious, even though she had merely sprinkled a few herbs on it and run it under the broiler. He liked being attended to, and feeling in an expansive mood as they sat at the wicker porch table in her alcove, Jonathan gratuitously offered her the information she was so desperately curious about. Myrna had responded with a little mewing sound, as if she were only mildly interested, and went on to say that the wine he had brought was lovely.

"So what does he do?" asked Sidney.

"Watch television and things."

" 'And things'? A likely story." When his information had produced so undramatic an effect on her, he had added that after the divorce he had gone through a period of quick, multiple, promiscuous relationships, and she had been most understanding about it.

"And he said he was glad that I asked him—actually glad. He didn't think I was being hostile or nosy." The palpitation of delight she felt when he answered her unasked question was dampened because at that precise moment she wasn't asking it. No look or gesture had betrayed her, although she had thought about it at length before he arrived and hoped the ambiance would encourage him. Giving herself the doorbell as a signal, she put the persistent issue from her mind. Dreading the thought that he was withholding the information from motives of secrecy, or that what was important to her might be of no consequence to him, she was glad when Jonathan had brought up his promiscuous interlude, because at some point he might ask her the number of people she had slept with, and no matter what she would tell him, like all men he would think it was too many.

"Yeah, but *were* you being hostile and nosy?"

"I don't blame you for asking me that dumb-dumb question. You're just trying to make me into a horrible barracuda so you can justify yourself for not having met me that night. And now that I've met someone marvelous, who cares about me, you can't stand it."

"Believe me, I can stand it," he said. "Can you?"

"Go ahead," she said indulgently. "You can't hurt me. I'm in love."

"Now. But how about next week?"

"I'm not afraid of the future any more," Myrna proclaimed. "You played it safe, and look where it's gotten you. You're still pressing your wet nose to the glass. But not this kid," she said, shaking her thumb at herself. "I'm not afraid of what will happen, and neither is he, in spite of what he's been through marriage-wise."

Jonathan hadn't planned on speaking so much about his ex-wife, but it was safer to talk about that than risk repeating something Sidney had told her on the telephone. Besides, as Jonathan he begrudged telling her anything he considered important about himself, because he might have the occasion to tell it to her as Sidney.

He was now leading a double life, when until recently he felt he lived only marginally in one. Whenever thoughts of the future demanded consideration, extrapolations of current events like figures at the bottom of a financial statement by which he advised his clients on coming fiscal quarters, Sidney balked at the idea that the same rigorous and predictable causality might govern his own life. Instead, he began to think in terms of the hazy, illogical incongruities that Myrna had tried to explain to him. He was contemptuous of them, but at the same time they offered such easy solutions because they absolved him of volition, particularly in the problem of Jonathan, which appeared to be insoluble whenever he thought about it. Then, shackled by the lines of force and tensions created by the stars and planets, he tried translating his relationship with Myrna into numbers, a kind of double-entry emotional bookkeeping, but the ambiguity of the dividends he was receiving refused to signify themselves as specific amounts, and he didn't like to think that his deception might be heading for bankrupcy. Having found Myrna through sheer chance, and having created his second self on the spur of the moment, he decided to proceed with no plan whatever.

Myrna had been most impressed by the two biggest lies he had invented about himself: his semi-orphan-hood and his broken marriage. Two women; one dead, one gone. Instinctively he knew that she needed him to be son and husband, identities at the edge of which her vast craving to love would flow like a current along a coastline. The profile of his masquerade had grown, ineluctably developed, the way a coast resisted and surrendered to the ocean, according to its inherent strengths and weaknesses. It seemed so right and natural to Sidney that he had given her the opportunity to exert her need to form him as Jonathan, making his malleability acceptable to himself by giving this need a maternal coloration. Acquiescence was easy, as long as she would protect him and take care of him in the bargain. The chicken had been excellent and she had been particularly inventive in bed.

While Myrna was making love to him, she couldn't escape the suspicion that he might be lying to her, and when he finally moved to return her favor, she had gently stopped him, as if to say that giving pleasure was all she wanted. In satisfying her curiosity, she had satisfied his lust; that was only fair. And she was convinced that what she had done for him in bed made what he said to her true.

"You make it sound as if Jonathan is the only person in the world who's had a hard time. He's got no monopoly on misery," Sidney said.

"But his is so much more interesting than yours. His misery could beat up your misery any day," she replied, remembering the terrible marital fights Jonathan had told her about and wondering if he'd ever hit his wife.

As she lay in Jonathan's arms she could see him, looking divine in dinner clothes and with a mustache that became him so, standing at the top of the spiral staircase, looking down at his wife, who stood slim as a knife, one jeweled hand on the balustrade, her head thrown back, exposing her white throat. She was laughing, triumphant, and as the sound echoed up into the beams of the cathedral ceiling of the Great Hall of Craythorne Manor, she told him she was with child, not his, and it was then he struck her full across the jagged, scarlet wound that was her mouth. She staggered back, her face a death mask, and then fell down the stairs and lay quite still at the bottom, a thin trickle of blood from the corner of her dead lips meandering over the black and white marble squares.

As he talked to her on the telephone, Sidney wondered whether Myrna believed in her new confidence and optimism, and knowing that her contempt for him was genuine, deep and abiding, he could not allow her to feel the security of any other unequivocal emotion. Perhaps if she doubted Jonathan, she might feel more charitable to him as Sidney. "Why would this fantastic person, who is so brilliant and everything, be sitting around watching television?" he asked.

"It's so marvelous to be in love," she said, as if ignoring him, "to know that somebody cares about you."

"Is that your definition?"

"Stop making me out to be so selfish. By the way, when was the last time anybody cared about you?"

It was his turn to ignore her. "Suppose he was seeing somebody else and *telling* you he was watching television?"

"I'm not the sort of person who could be in love with a liar."

Myrna wished she had a mirror just then, so she might see whether her expression showed the same conviction she hoped was apparent in her voice. Could he be a liar, she wondered. What about all the times she had lied to make herself more desirable to him? What about the times she had feigned interest in what he said, thought, felt, seen, experienced—were those lies? And when he had spoken to her about his ex-wife, when all she wanted from him was an indication that he needed her, and she had nodded in agreement when she had wanted to cry out that she would be different —that wasn't a lie, or was it?

She had given him signals instead of simple facts, sidelong glances as placebos for a single clear-eyed look. That was part of the game, not lying. Was it deceitful not to have told him he'd have to lose ten pounds, when her hand caressed his back where it met his hip and she felt the flesh swell where it should have been tight smooth? And was it a lie when she had not told him to please do it just a bit longer, frightened that he would think she was making a demand on him, telling herself she was more concerned with his ego than her own pleasure?

With little difficulty she convinced herself that he made her do these things, and also that her sins were mainly omissive, telling herself there was a big difference between lying and not telling the truth. While Jonathan made her do these things, it did not mean that he could not love her, or would not love her, if she'd only take the initiative and tell him the truth. Then he could not fail to love her, because—she fairly glowed with the revelation—she could never tell him the truth without his loving her in the first place.

"It doesn't make any difference anyway," Sidney said. "I don't see much difference between his watching television and going out with another girl. They're both *not* going out with you."

"I wouldn't expect you to distinguish between a live person and a television set." Click.

Sidney lay on his bed, a numbness growing within him like a fatal disease. The lifeless receiver still dangled by the night table. He breathed heavily to exhale the pain, but as he drew another breath, he was aware that he only sucked in part of the emptiness that surrounded him. Crossing to the window, he opened it, inhaling and exhaling, seeing his breath condensing as a gray vapor in the winter air. But it vanished, and with it the feeling that he was alive. From the drawer of the night table he took the notebook he had been keeping, and reread the jottings he had made about himself; it had been stupid telling her about the boat, even though it was only twenty-two feet long, and now he would have to tell her he'd sold it. If only she hadn't mentioned the weekend sail she had been on the summer before, he would not have invented it.

Turning off the light, waiting for sleep, he debated whether he ought to kill off Sidney or Jonathan, unable to decide if he could be the object of her contempt or her love. But the two personae were joined together like Siamese twins, sharing one set of vital organs, and though they loathed each other, pulling in opposite directions, they were ultimately forced to give up the struggle as the point of contact began to tear and bleed.

•   •   •

"It's Sidney. How are you?"

"Terrible. Jonathan and I had a rather difficult discussion."

"You mean fight."

"Okay, fight!"

"I'll bet he's a tiger when roused," Sidney said.

"Oh, don't be that way tonight. I'm not in the mood."

Betrayed. She betrayed me, Sidney thought. "What did you fight about?"

"It's not *what* we fought about that's important. It's that it seems we have a really very basic difference in life style. You think you know somebody, and suddenly they reveal a side of themselves you never dreamed was there. I've got a suspicion that Jonathan is actually rather tight-assed at heart. If there's anything I can't stand, it's a rigid person."

"Well, you met him at a difficult time—I mean for him. He was recently divorced, so maybe he's not ready for a meaningful relationship."

"Oh Christ, is it my fault he got divorced? Did I tell him to marry her? That's all he ever talks about."

Everything Jonathan had done the night before had annoyed her; all the mannerisms and idiosyncrasies, the base metals of life that were supposed to be transformed into lovers' gold, seemed odd and distasteful to her. Sidney had been right. There wasn't much difference between what he was doing on alternative nights. As she looked at his contentment after their Mexican dinner, she wished he'd stop with the fun-food and take her for a decent steak the next time. Again he had the power; she might silently propose, but he would eventually dispose, she hoped. It was maddening, but even more maddening was the possibility, as before, that he didn't realize he could use the power she gave him. His smile and the touch of his hand didn't prove a thing. Smiling back and pressing the hand that was so sweaty in hers, she nearly moaned in frustration and uncertainty. She searched, as she had with other men, for the way to bring him back into phase with her own accelerating expectations. No more fox trots; there was no time for building slowly, for enigmatic silences, for talking about ideas, the world—at least any part of the world that did not directly concern her. A full stomach seemed to enlarge his interests, instead of removing hunger as an obstacle to his being entirely focused on her.

She might find a way of surviving Jonathan's post-prandial discourses on the population explosion, or the threat to the great osprey, and while she was deeply and sincerely interested in these problems, Myrna only thought about how she might turn him inward again, to her, to them. The recounting of the small incidents of her life, told again by her with considerable effort, trailing a wake of other faces who had listened, other beds, other disappointments, had brought them this far. What she needed now was instant intimacy, which like a shock treatment would break through the barrier that separated them.

"Why are you making excuses for him?" she said to Sidney. "What about me?"

"I don't know. Maybe you're going too fast for him. Don't get so hysterical. If I knew what you were fighting about, maybe I could give you my opinion," he said, wanting her to tell him what she had done and why.

"It's simply a question of how people handle their negative feelings. What I want to know is *why* he's being so hostile to me. All I do is sit around fulfilling all *his* needs and adjusting. Why have I always got to be the one who adjusts?" Since Myrna had met Jonathan, the premeditation with which she prepared herself for their meetings had begun to take its toll. When she had massaged the cream into her body the night before, it was as if she were covering up the cracks that were beginning to open, like the veneer on an old chest of drawers. If she could be sure of him, she would have waited, but impulsively she decided to take the initiative. Not only would she reveal herself; she would divulge a secret in spite of which he would love her. But when she told Jonathan about Sidney, it hadn't worked out that way.

"I guess everyone goes through these periods of doubt. It's only natural," Sidney reassured her, unable to accept the idea that Myrna might come to hate Jonathan too.

"I'm frightened. I'm frightened, Sidney. I've got a chance to be happy," she said, sounding as if it were her last. "I mean I *am* happy, and I want to keep it that way. Sidney, I think I did something terrible. I told Jonathan about us."

It was as if he knew it for the first time. Betrayed. She had betrayed him, and now she expected him to be her ally. "I told you nobody would understand," Sidney blurted out. "What did he say?"

"He said he thought it was a very sick thing."

For once she was quoting him correctly. My God, he thought, she is telling me the truth. He had sat, horror-stricken, as if listening to an obscene confession, while Myrna had told him. Anxious to hear how she would describe him and her feelings, he had permitted her to go on, caught between wanting to hear about himself again and knowing she was using him. When Myrna saw the look of dismay and indignation on his face that he fought to control, she kept saying that she knew it was unbelievable, but Sidney was perfectly harmless. The third time she said it, he asked her how she could be so sure this pervert was so harmless, and she had told him again that she was certain he didn't even know where she lived, as she repeated, laughing nervously, that he found her number scrawled on the seat of a bus.

"Do *you* think it's sick?" Sidney demanded.

"It doesn't matter whether I do or don't, it's what he thinks that matters. After all, who am I?" she asked. "A poor slob looking to get married. Sidney," she pleaded, "what am I going to do? I can't let this one get away. I can't go through this crap again. I'm so tired of telling about when I was four. I was insane to think that anybody could care about me. Why doesn't anybody give me a chance to love them? Doesn't anyone care about love any more," she cried, feeling she had outlived her time.

Maybe she had made a big mistake. Older men were the solution—really older, about seventy-five, someone who read books, wife dead—better than alive and divorced—whose children had long grown and gone away, and she would sit quietly in the library, the great mastiff lounging at his feet while he quoted Gibbon and Thucydides when he wasn't telling her how fond he was of her.

I can't tell her that she's had her chance with me, Sidney thought, not daring to say that he cared about love, for fear that in her anger toward Jonathan she would take him at his word, clutch at him, the last straw. As Jonathan he had almost asked her whether she thought Sidney had any feelings for her, but instead had only demanded if they had ever met. No, she had answered, what did he take her for? Of course she would have omitted that episode, and in a way he had a slight satisfaction. At least he knew his disapproval meant something, even though Myrna had then let it be known that she thought Jonathan was being ever so slightly conventional in his reproaches of her. When she made the most oblique reference to his ex-wife, intimating faintly that he might not be one hundred percent normal, he had taken considerable umbrage. Wasn't she satisfied that he had described his ex as an insufferable shit? There wasn't any cause to bring her into this. He didn't think it was mature to be bitter about the past. Myrna subsided into an uneasy truce, while he thought how pleasant it was to be able to intimidate her with the threat of withdrawing his approbation, and thereby, her hopes.

"Did you ask him why he was so upset?" Sidney asked.

"If you went out with a girl and she told you she was practically having an affair with a telephone pervert, what would you say?" she asked.

"If I didn't love you and you told me, then I'd say you were out of your mind; on the other hand, if I did love you and you told me, I'd tell you that you were out of your mind—but then, if I loved you I'd be out of my mind."

"You're a big help."

"What are you making such a drama about? You talk as if Jonathan is the last one to come down the pike."

"Sidney darling, I am exactly thirty-six and a half years old. I have never been married, and if you want to hear something I've never told a living soul, I've never even had an abortion. Now that's how out of it I am. I'm too old for spending my life in restaurants eating greaseball food. I want to talk about what happened in the playground, not about whether we should send astronauts to Mars. Do I give a damn? Sometimes when I'm coming home from work, I want to lie down in the street and curl up, I'm so weary. You know why I don't?

Because some goddamn person would come along with a poodle and stand there while he pissed on me."

"The person?"

"This is no time to correct my syntax. Look, I'll admit to you Jonathan is no big, fat bargain. He's a nice, sweet guy. Did I tell you, he's got this gorgeous boat. It sounds like something out of *Playboy*. Stereo and everything. I forget how many feet, but it sleeps four." Would there be a summer of sun and glittering water, or merely the days growing hotter and longer? "Sidney, what am I going to do?" she said. "I've got to do something."

Advising Myrna about his own seduction was not as easy as it should have been. "You *are* doing something. You're eating with him. You're sleeping with him. That's doing something." It was unpleasant hearing himself being described as a nice, sweet guy. "But there's no question that Jonathan is in a superior position. Let's face it, either you go along, smiling through your tears, or you risk blowing the whole scene. I know it sounds unfair, but if I were in his place, I'd figure it that way. Here's a guy who's just gotten out of one lousy relationship, so now all he wants is something that's easy and non-sweat-making."

"So I'm supposed to sit there being a dear little mouse, while he gets his jollies."

"You're not *supposed* to do anything. I'm simply pointing out one way of keeping the relationship going, which is what you seem to want. What I want to know is why you told him about us in the first place. You must have been completely nuts. I told you nobody would understand. Why don't you ever listen to me?"

"I wanted to tell him the worst thing about myself.

I figured if he knew that, he'd have to love me. Don't you see; he'd have to love me because I told him. It was so simple."

"Why didn't you tell him about the girl whose wedding you didn't go to. That's the worst thing I ever heard."

"But then he got this stricken look, and then I started to say things like 'Well, it's not so terrible,' and things like that, justifying what I'd done, when all I wanted him to say was that he did think it was disgusting but he'd forgive me. Then I'd fall at his feet and clasp him around the knees and he'd raise me up in his strong arms, kiss my tear-stained face crimson with shame, and then he'd give me his mother's brooch."

"Say that again," Sidney said, not sure he had heard her correctly.

"I thought maybe he'd want to protect me, and that we'd start seeing each other every night so that I *couldn't* talk to you even if I wanted to."

"From what you told me," Sidney said, "he sounds like a very strong person, with very definite ideas, but maybe he feels he doesn't have the right to tell you what to do and not to do. Maybe that's one of the things he found out about his marriage."

"Jesus, you're almost as bad as he is. At first I liked the idea that he'd been married before, but I'm getting a wee bit annoyed now."

"Jonathan obviously still has emotional connections with that part of his life; you wouldn't want it any other way, would you? If he could forget an entire marriage so soon, it would mean that he didn't have any emotional life at all."

"That's true. That's true, isn't it?"

Reluctantly, Sidney agreed. All she needed was a little psychic hook on which to hang her expectations, like dresses waiting to be worn.

"You're very smart, Sidney," she said. "Now let me ask you this: Do you or do you not think that Jonathan will start to see me every night, and if so, when?"

In making excuses for Jonathan, Sidney expected to gain points at both ends, but he saw he was wrong. "How do I know," he answered angrily. "Go look it up in your horoscope. You're never satisfied. I've straightened out your romance for you and all you want is more. How do you think I feel when you keep telling me about him all the time? Maybe you don't think I've got feelings, but I do. It's very hard to listen to what he said and what you said. You told him about us. You *told!*"

"Why do you keep coming back to that."

"Because it was something we shared together, that was just ours. Don't you feel you're betraying Jonathan when you tell me about him?"

"I would if I was sure he loved me."

"If you loved me, would you have told Jonathan anyway?"

"If I loved you, I wouldn't be going out with Jonathan in the first place," she said.

"So what you're saying is that you don't love me, and you're not sure whether Jonathan loves you. But you haven't said whether you love Jonathan, or whether you would betray him regardless of the way you felt. I know that you'd betray me if you didn't love me, because you already have."

"I don't admit that I betrayed anybody. I tell you, Sidney, if he doesn't get on the stick pretty soon, the whole thing is off."

"Don't threaten *me*," Sidney said, "threaten him. What are you taking it out on me for?"

"You play Jonathan, and I'll be myself, and we'll have a scene where I ask you what your story is with this business about seeing me every night."

"What do I call you?"

"Never mind about that. You ready? Okay. 'Look, Jonathan, I've got something I must talk to you about.'" A silence. "So? . . . what are you doing?"

"I'm looking at you with interest."

"'I've got to know what's going to be with us.'" Another silence. "What are you *doing*, for Christ's sake?"

"I'm thinking."

"If you've got to think about it, I can't mean that much to you. I don't want to play any more." Click.

• • •

"Hello, it's Sidney. How are you?"

"Not bad."

He had expected her to say that she was fabulous, at least. "Not good?"

"Actually, pretty good," Myrna admitted. "Jonathan told me last night that he had given considerable thought to our relationship on the phone, and he felt that he had no right to approve or disapprove of it. He said if I thought it was meaningful, that was up to me."

"But that didn't satisfy you."

"Well, yes and no. I liked the idea that he had thought about it, but I was hoping he'd tell me some hideous thing about himself so that we would be even and then I could love him in spite of himself."

"It's possible that he doesn't have anything hideous to tell you. Or maybe he wasn't aware that's what you wanted from him."

"Why not? He's supposed to be aware of things like that."

"It seems to me that you've changed your tune since last week," Sidney said. "I can't figure out why you want to be with Jonathan if you've got all these complaints."

"I don't mean to say that he's not fantastic, because he is; it's that some of his fantasticness isn't that fantastic. You know I like somebody who is very strong and assertive, but when he says something like 'Waiter,' to the waiter, his voice drops about two octaves and it sounds like he's about to recite the Gettysburg Address. You ought to be able to say something like that and not make such a big deal about it."

Now she was complaining about his delivery. "That's a very small detail," he said, "considering the picture as a whole. If you can be so carping about one mannerism, it doesn't seem to me that you could be all that hot for him in the first place."

"You're amazing, Sidney. Sometimes you're so perceptive, like the night before last, and other times you don't have the faintest inkling of what goes on between two people. The point is, it's because I am so hot for him, as you so delicately put it, that I can admit to myself that he's not perfection. Don't you see that's the mark of a mature relationship?"

"But you didn't only admit it to yourself; you admitted it to me."

"But that's like talking to myself," she said, rushing past the idea that he was almost a part of her. "It's very comforting to talk to somebody about this."

"Why don't you talk to Jonathan about the way you feel?"

"Oh, Sidney, honestly. You sound as if you'd never been involved with anyone. You can't go spewing out everything if you're going to be devastatingly attractive. Do you think I'd be idiot enough to tell Jonathan I didn't like the way he said waiter. No—because you've got to decide what you can live with and what you can't, and I've decided."

"It sounds like you have reservations."

"This is a very exclusive place. You can't get in without reservations," she said. "The other night I was thinking that I'd be willing to spend my entire life with him, even if I didn't love him, providing I could be absolutely sure I wouldn't ever hate him."

"You're entitled to something more," Sidney said. "Everybody is."

"But then I started to wonder whether he might want to marry me for the same reason, and if so, whether I would marry him, knowing that."

"For a romantic type, you've been doing a lot of thinking and figuring."

"A girl in my position . . ."

"I liked it better when you were swooning with delight instead of being so calculating and analytical, even

)) 176

though I suspected that part of it was for my benefit."

"What are you going to do with your life, by the way?"

Coming from her, the question surprised him. "I don't know," said Sidney. "Let it happen."

"Just like that? How? I'm not always going to be here for you, you know."

"Who said you were? Where are you going to be, if I may be so bold as to ask? I'm aware that you're using me. You need me. But let's not get into who's the dependent one. For some reason you're not satisfied with this guy who is: one, handsome; two, fascinating; three, a great lover—just because he doesn't say waiter right. What exactly is it that you have to adjust to, for Christ's sake? He's the one who has to adjust to you; a guy like that could have anyone. I frankly don't see why he's going out with you at all, and you're psyched up about why he isn't seeing you every night. So you use me to make him want you more, and then you come to me and complain that your plan isn't working."

"He's not that great-looking."

"What do you mean?"

"Of course, he's not Quasimodo either."

"And he's not fascinating?"

"I wouldn't exactly say *fascinating*. He's more like interesting."

"I don't want to hear about the sex part."

"I can't remember it very well from one time to the next, but I suppose that's my fault."

"At least *something's* your fault."

"It's all my fault—you're my fault; he's my fault. Everything's my fault. Everybody I've ever met has brought out the worst in me. They're all so defensive. What are they defending themselves against? What do they think I'm going to do to them?"

Rather than answer her questions, he said, "Don't panic. I'm sure you've got a lot of very positive feelings for Jonathan, like you had when you met him for the first time."

"It's funny his disapproving of you, when I'd never have met him otherwise. I didn't tell him about that, not after the way he reacted to the telephone part. I don't know why you don't disapprove of him; you're supposed to be jealous."

"I guess I never believed Jonathan was as marvelous as you said he was."

"There's one thing that is marvelous about him, and that is he's alive, and around. I'm not going to hang around and wait for Mr. Wonderful. Right now I've got Mr. Adequate."

"Not quite."

"Okay, at least every other night. That's pretty depressing when I think about it."

"Stop thinking."

"Believe me, I'd like to, but there's something about Jonathan that makes me very rational. You know, when I was twenty-two, twenty-three, I used not to think, or adjust, or anything. I had my own apartment and all, and naturally I got broken up about my star-crossed affairs, but I could say okay, sombody else will be turning up. So if I didn't like the way he wore his hat, the way he sang off key, I could say goodbye, and then I'd stay very still and wait for my life to begin again. I remember I had this terrific fight with somebody about a movie—a *movie*— would you believe it? I remember the fight but not the picture. I said, 'Look, obviously we can't go on seeing each other, if you don't like . . . I don't know what . . . *Francis Goes to College*, or some goddamn thing. Now when Jonathan says 'Waiter,' " Myrna mimicked, her voice dropping to a contralto, "I think to myself, Cool it—even though it drives me insane."

"You're not going to find anyone who doesn't have at least one mannerism . . . except maybe me. I don't have a single habit. I'm mass-produced."

"The stupid thing is that Jonathan is my big throb, and he's the one who makes me think and get all involved in maybe's and might's and what-if's and all that stuff. And you, Sidney the Accountant, are the one who's letting me not think. I don't think about the future with you."

But the future has already happened, Sidney thought. "Jonathan is beginning a new life with you," he said. "He probably wouldn't admit it, but my guess is that you're probably the first woman he's been with since his divorce."

"Do you really think so?"

"I wouldn't be a bit surprised, from the way you talk. You say he talks about his ex-wife a lot?"

"A *lot* isn't the word for it," she replied.

"It sounds like he's trying to defend himself against his true feelings—almost as if he were very involved with you and wanted somehow to exorcise the past."

Troubled footsteps, his footsteps, had echoed along the gallery that led to the West Wing, and through the door of the bedchamber she had seen him in the long brocaded dressing gown, walking with measured steps toward the door that had always been locked, and for which she didn't have the key. A shriek sounded in the night, or was it merely the wind tearing at the gables? As she stepped onto the gallery, he turned, facing her, and she saw that he was wearing an incredibly boring tie, just like the one Jonathan had on the night before.

"It doesn't work any more," Myrna said.

"What doesn't work?" asked Sidney.

"Never mind. I think the real world is closing in on me. Sidney! Don't hang up. I mean don't hang up at all tonight. I don't want to be alone tonight. Not tonight."

The unexpected plea frightened him, and as if attacked, he switched the receiver to the other ear.

Myrna wondered what Jonathan might be doing at that moment, but checked the impulse to ask Sidney's opinion. "I don't want to think about it," she said.

"You're not making sense," he said.

"I can't be alone tonight. I can't."

"You're not alone. You've got me."

"You keep saying that," Myrna answered. "Then don't hang up."

"It's late."

"I can't ask you again."

"Are you ready for bed?"

"I've got to put some stuff on my face."

"I've got to brush my teeth. I'll be back in five minutes."

"Do you brush each one individually?"

"I've also got to go to the john. Okay, four minutes."

Myrna rose from the bed, went to the bureau drawer and selected a light-blue tricot nightgown with a halter neck that Helen Gurley Brown said would do wonders for her breasts. In the welter of bottles, spray cans and lipsticks, she found a soft plastic container, which she squeezed, excreting a thick glob of hormone-enriched oil that she rubbed between her hands and applied from the bridge of her nose outward in long even strokes. Wiping off the excess, she returned to the bed, picked up the receiver lying on the pillow and listened. As she heard a sudden rush of water in the background, she turned down the covers and got in, holding the phone next to her ear.

Sidney turned off the light in the bathroom and stood briefly on the threshold, looking at the phone on his bed. The beige forms with their rounded corners connected by twisted unbilical wire seemed like a weird, hairless creature who had given birth to an even stranger mutation with two perforated extremities turned toward him, two eyes. A cool wetness touched his leg where a few errant drops stained his pajamas. Carefully picking up the receiver, he placed the folded handkerchief over the mouthpiece and listened. "You there?" he said.

"Yeah."

"I'm turning off my light," he said, reaching for the lamp on the night table. Instantly the room was completely dark. Then the familiar outlines of the furniture returned as his eyes became accustomed to the glow of light from the street.

"Mine's off too," Myrna said, turning to flick off her lamp. The table lamp inadvertently left on in the living room sent a slice of brightness across the floor, and from where she lay she could see the openwork shadows of the furniture and part of a white chair that stood dis-

181 ((

consolately, like a patient in a clinic. Turning away and pressing the receiver close to her ear, she said, "What time do you get up for work?"

"The alarm's set for seven-thirty. I take a shower in the morning."

"I take mine at night."

"Don't you feel grubby beginning the day without a shower?"

"I can't stand water on me at that hour. I'm fine once I've got my make-up on. When you get up, don't say anything. Just hang up."

"Right," he said, shifting his weight, shaping the pillow and grunting as he rearranged the covers.

"What are you doing?"

"I'm trying to get comfortable. I've never slept with a telephone before."

"Did you ever notice how warm telephones are? They must use a special plastic." Myrna said, cradling the receiver in her neck.

How lovely it would be to stay like this forever, she thought, feeling how easily the phone fit into the hollow, and of all the knees and elbows that had crowded her in bed over the years, the heavy satisfied bodies that breathed and murmured and coughed while she had stared into the darkness, wondering and waiting. Now the warmth spread over her, as if she were taking a nap in the evening after coming home from work: a little lie-down that stretched into timeless, indulgent surrender to tiredness—not washing her hair, not working on her photographs—drugged, jellied, floating on a tropical sea. The delicious weightlessness passed as she remembered how Jonathan had lain on top of her after they had made love the night before, massive and impenetrable as he dozed, still between her legs, his breath smelling of wine and the hand that lay on the pillow exuding the aroma of her femaleness. He slipped away from her while his torso pinned her, and to distract herself from a persistent apprehension inside her, Myrna had explored, lightly, so as not to wake him, the damp secret crease of his behind, as if she would find the answer there without his knowing it.

Gently she put the receiver down next to her, and arching her body, drew the slippery nightgown over her head, letting it fall beside the bed.

"I wonder how many message units this is going to cost me," Sidney said. But there was no answer.

His thoughts shuttled between Jonathan and himself. The inevitable was happening the more he was with Myrna, and not even her romanticism, her clamoring willingness to transform his dense, unremarkable reality would change that. Occasionally he had been able to think of Jonathan as separate and distinct, as long as she described him as he wanted to be, but her disenchantment had brought him back. There was no escape from himself, except if he helped her, supported her, turned her disappointments into signs of hope, read legends into Jonathan's silences, gave deep meanings to his hesitant, fragmentary confidences as they sat at dinner or lay in bed.

Jonathan was her creation as much as his. Mouthing "Waiter" almost audibly, he wondered what would please her, attempting to invent another facet of his past that might endear Jonathan to her: the time he had been on safari, a rare disease. Feeling that his own identity had diluted all the other colorful inventions he had offered, Sidney knew that only something extreme would do. Consequences and effects eluded him as he planned, and whenever a feeble warning sounded that he might not be able to cope with yet another lie, an admonition that try as he might, he could only *appear* different rather than *be* different, a hint that whatever he invented, however bizarre and outlandish, could only emanate from his strangling imagination, he took heart in the idea that at least he was getting laid a couple of times a week.

Myrna complained about her position, Sidney thought—but what about his? At least she had a plan, an objective, but knowing what she wanted of him made it no less difficult to decide whether he would allow her to succeed. Realistically, he would have to find some way of dealing with the routine that had evolved, knowing that before long, contrary to his advice, she would begin to feel victimized again. And yet if he began seeing her every night, what would become of him, both of him? Once having achieved that interim goal, she would press him for another concession, another payment of tribute; she towered before him, a demanding empress. Again the feeling of having been betrayed by her suffused him, and the knowledge that she would readily eviscerate him to read his entrails if she thought it augured well for her future.

But the anger stilled in him as sleep approached, leaving him cold and burned out, ashen, and Sidney drew the covers closer around him, folding himself into a compact mass to be more concentrated, more substantial. "You awake?" he said.

As he lay holding the phone, listening for a response, it seemed as if nothing he had ever felt or thought had had any effect, nor that any action resulting from those feelings or thoughts had left the slightest mark on any-body or anything. It had been foolish to think that Myrna was his creation; she was proceeding on her own, drawing strength from the unchangeable, tangible stuff of her identity, and as he saw her in his mind with the utmost clarity, Sidney knew it was not his vision that focused her so precisely, but her adamant, insistent, enviable actuality. He could see the curling wisps of her brown hair, her prominent nose askew like a tassel disturbed by a gust of wind, and her dark valiant eyes. "Are you awake?" he said, louder. There was no reply. "Margaret, Mary, Maxine," he began, softly recit-ing the names he had called her, and then, putting his hand over the receiver, he said, "Goodnight, Myrna."

• • •

"Hello."
"Hello, Sidney."
"How'd you sleep the other night?"
"Fine. How'd you?"
"Fine, except I had a funny feeling when I woke up and saw the receiver next to me in the bed."
"Yeah, me too," she said, thinking it was like finding the perfect lover, still hard and smooth from the night before. "Did you listen?"
"I was going to, but then I just hung up. That's what you told me to do." He hadn't listened, but he had lain

in bed after hanging up, as if it were Sunday, and for a half hour imagined Myrna preparing herself for the day. "I didn't talk in my sleep or snore or anything, did I?"

"I don't know. I went right out like a light."

"I thought about you a lot yesterday, while I was at work. A guy at the office came up to me and said I looked like I had a very good night, or a very bad night."

"Did you think about me last night?"

Sidney laughed.

"It's a perfectly normal question. I'm not getting into the same scene with you as I am with Jonathan."

"Wouldn't you rather know *what* I was thinking?"

"Now you have to tell me where you were too."

"Well, after I came home from the office and showered and got into my tuxedo, I had a drink with Raquel Welch . . ."

"Come on."

"I thought about you when I was watching the Late Show."

"A likely story."

"And *then* I had a drink with Raquel Welch."

"Very funny, very funny. You and Jonathan certainly lead the most fascinating lives when you're not with me."

"I don't see why you wouldn't believe that I could get a date with somebody like Raquel Welch."

"For the same reason you didn't believe that Jonathan was the way I described him to you."

"That's different. Jonathan is a real person."

"Sometimes I wonder," she said. "I'm beginning to think I made him up entirely."

"What's the matter. What's happening?"

"Nothing. That's the point. It's all dwindling away like the sand in one of those timers you get for a three-minute egg."

"So turn him over and start all over again."

"Anyway, he sold his boat. He told me last night. Are you ready?" she said, pausing before the punch line. "He's decided to take up sports-car racing."

"That sounds very exciting. I think it takes a lot of guts."

"A boat is something two people can sit on, and relax on, and screw on under the stars. I don't intend to go tooling around in an oversized kiddie car just so he can show off his guts, which are getting a little flabby."

"I would have thought you'd be thrilled with the idea."

"Maybe I would have a week or so ago, when I was into how great he was. He seemed kind of annoyed that I wasn't too enthusiastic about his new hobby, so I told him I didn't like the idea of his getting maimed or killed or something."

"You mean it was just the idea you didn't like."

"So he tells me that life is full of chances, and that's what makes it exciting. That's his big discovery, like when all the time I'm taking an enormous chance with him."

"You're telling me that the possibility of getting broken into a thousand pieces and not getting married are the same thing."

"Well?"

"The more you talk about Jonathan's faults, the more he sounds like the guy you originally met. He sounds great."

"Why the hell are you being so sympathetic to him?"

"I'm not. I just want what's best for you."

"I still haven't heard a peep out of him about seeing me every night."

"Nobody announces something like that; it'll happen, that's all. One day he'll say, 'I'll see you tomorrow night.' "

"I was wondering about it last night, and I thought that if we started seeing each other all the time, I wouldn't have a chance to talk to you. Maybe I'd better give you my number at work, just in case."

"What will happen after you're married? I suppose you'll want me to call you during the day while Jonathan is breaking his ass at the office."

"It wouldn't exactly be like being unfaithful."

"Did it ever occur to you that I might meet somebody and get married?"

The idea did seem odd to her. "Sidney, are you trying to tell me something? What's she like? No, don't tell me. I don't want to know."

"There isn't anybody else besides you. That's the truth."

"I know you wouldn't ever lie to me."

"No," he said weakly, succumbing to a spasm of guilt, the first since he had become Jonathan. Involuntarily closing his eyes, he felt the vertigo he knew had been waiting for him all along.

"That's beautiful. I wish I could say the same about myself."

"Don't think about that. You'll get hurt that way. Just think about what works for you. I don't want you to get hurt."

"You're such a deep person, Sidney, such a good person. Jesus, I never thought I'd hear myself saying that. Maybe I ought to break up with Jonathan," Myrna offered, thinking that then Sidney could call her every night, like he used to, and there would be no complications, "and then . . ."

"That's no solution," he broke in. "You once thought you could love him. Maybe you even did and didn't know it. You'll feel that way again."

"How will I tell if I didn't know it before? And what about you?"

"Never mind about me. You've got to be happy. Somebody's got to be happy," he said, implusively offering himself as sacrifice, suddenly sick to death of his masquerade, but even more revolted by himself, grasping at the hope that her love, that huge thing in her that had always frightened him so, might once again revive Jonathan in all his first glory.

"I'll try," she said, as though he had asked her to do the impossible.

•   •   •

"Hello, it's Sidney."

"Oh God, Sidney, I'm so glad you called." There was

a breathy urgency to her voice. "Something incredible has happened."

He went over the events of the last evening with her, quickly at first, then in detail, knowing that she was capable of making much out of nothing but still confused that such an uneventful time could have produced such a dramatic aftereffect. Absolutely nothing out of the ordinary had occurred. Immediately he knew she had prepared an elaborate lie: she was going to tell him that Jonathan had asked her out that night and she had just gotten home from being with him when he called. Well, she wasn't going to get away with it. "What happened?" he asked, trying not to reveal his anger.

"Oh, Sidney," she said, her voice ringing with joy, "I was out with Jonathan last night, and we went through our usual routine, with dinner and the rest of it, and later he began to talk again about that goddamn new car he was getting, and I was lying there and I felt a tight little smile on my face. And I just stopped smiling. I can't tell you what a relief it was. And then suddenly, *suddenly* he seemed like a completely different person. I was looking at him and I said to myself, Why have I been getting so upset about *this?* I knew instantly that he never really wanted to know anything about me, and that I couldn't ever tell him, not the way I've told you."

Sidney had never heard such a vibrant resonance in her voice before, not even in the early days with Jonathan.

"There isn't anything I wouldn't tell you now, Sidney. You've been the only one who has ever cared about me, seen me the way I really am and cared anyway. I don't have to adjust with you. So then I got up and made coffee, like I usually do, and we sat in the living room, as usual, and looked at each other, not saying anything, and I realized that he never *had* said anything, not to me at least. Oh God, Sidney, how could I have been so stupid not to see, not to see that you've been the only one who's ever cared about me, the only one who has ever offered to sacrifice himself for my happiness. Nobody has ever done that before." She stopped to catch her breath. "Sidney, it's you. I don't have to think about it because I know it's true. I can feel it! Sidney, it's you I love. I love you!" Her voice had risen to an exultant sob. "It's you, you. Sidney, do you hear me?" she said anxiously to the silence. "Sidney! I love you. My name is Myrna."

Sidney changed the receiver to his other ear. The room went out of focus, and after a moment he hung up the telephone.

ABOUT THE AUTHOR

A native New Yorker, PETER MARKS attended Amherst College, where he majored in European history. Following a career as a graphic designer, he opened a private gallery of Near Eastern and Oriental antiquities, and now travels frequently beyond the Bosphorus in search of art objects for museums and collectors. His first novel, *Collector's Choice*, published last year, dealt with the byzantine machinations of the art world, and work now in progress includes a book about American sculpture and a third novel. He lives in New York with his wife and three children.